JESSICA

A YOUNG WOMAN'S JOURNEY

RICHARD LEE

Dedicated to a world in need of love and imagination.

"Men are all alike - except the one you've met who's different." - Mae West

CONTENTS

FOREWORD

Jessica is a twenty-year-old music student in the second year of her studies.

It is the first time she has lived away from her home town of Armidale and she discovers that Sydney is a most exciting place to be. This is her story.

PREFACE

"We might start with the slutty shoes, darling. Although maybe they won't be too slutty. The sooner you get to practice walking in heels, the easier it will become."

Jessica let out a scream.

"You're really serious about this aren't you. You just want to make me into a bloody lipstick lesbian. I know where this is going."

— from Mount Eros

JESSICA MEETS ROSA

Rosa turned and looked at the young person standing not far away and looking a little lost. At first she though it was a young lad – one of the choirboys staying in the house – but when Rosa looked closer, she saw that it was a rather tomboyish young woman.

The young woman looked back at her. Since Rosa was no longer engaged in conversation with anyone, she moved over to her.

"So! I don't think we've met. My name is Rosa. What is yours?"

The slightly nervous girl smiled and said her name was Jessica and that she was a music student from Armidale and had come with her aunt and uncle that morning to stay with Maude for the weekend. She was feeling a bit out of place here and wished she had stayed at home.

Rosa eyed her new young friend keenly.

"No, Jessica! Being here is a good thing because, especially at your age, new experiences are very important. I remember how I felt awkward when I was younger and my parents had to make me go to things. Life is a bit like learning the piano, really. You hate the practice but love it later on when you can dash off the Moonlight Sonata and impress everyone."

Jessica smiled for the first time and Rosa was rewarded by seeing this slightly unusual creature relax a little. Jessica was quite tall and very thin and showed no sign of developing breasts. Her hair was auburn and her face reminded Rosa of one of those Pre-Raphaelite paintings of young women, serene and beautiful and with a far-away look in their eyes. The girl's movements were slow and graceful, but Rosa couldn't put an age to her and only guessed that she could be anywhere between fifteen and twenty-five.

"There you are, Jessica. Thought we'd lost you, darling!"

Rosa turned and looked at a woman in her fifties who, despite the hot weather, was wearing a cardigan over a woollen dress, heavy grey lisle stockings and solid brown brogues. Her manner was constrained and she seemed a little hesitant when she spoke.

"Oh no, Auntie. I'm not lost. I was trying to do what you suggested and circulate. I have just met this beautiful lady. Rosa? This is my aunt Edith who is the wife of mum's brother, the Reverend Cameron."

The two women looked at each other keenly and shook hands.

"Very pleased to meet you Rosa. I take it you are a friend of Maude?"

Rosa noticed that both aunt and niece made furtive glances at her hands and feet. Were they both fascinated with her lipstick perhaps, and her red-painted finger and toenails?

"Yes, we've known each other for many years and, until just recently, Maude has stayed with us on her monthly visits to town. Do you get to Sydney often, Edith?"

"Not often enough, unfortunately, Rosa. Getting away from one's husband isn't easy when you live that far away from the city. I've also been the librarian at a girls private school for many years but I will retire from that post next month.

"Getting away is not easy, but I'm planning to change things a bit if Jessica decides that she wants to come and board here. If she does, then I'll try to get down regularly to be with her. Unless of course she suddenly gets a boyfriend and doesn't want me hanging about."

The three women chuckled, enjoying the joke, but Rosa was thinking ahead. She had noticed that, although Edith laughed as she talked about getting away from her husband, she wasn't laughing inside; and having watched the Reverend Cameron talking to a man earlier at fairly close range, she had taken an instant dislike to him.

It was obvious, too, that Jessica represented a lifeline for Edith's escape from her country prison and maybe – just maybe – there was something more to the older woman's attentiveness towards her niece.

It was very hot in the room, partly because of the outside summer heat and also because of the large number of people. Jessica swished her skirt about to make a breeze and said how hot it was. Then she looked at her aunt and told Edith that she "must be boiling in all those clothes".

The impish and sensual Rosa began to plot. She took a risk.

"I'm feeling so hot that I'm thinking that I will go and find an empty unit where I can slip out of this dress and lie on a bed under a ceiling fan. Are either of you interested in joining me?"

The silence went on for so long that Rosa thought neither of the women had heard her. Just when she was about to rephrase the invitation, Jessica whispered "Yes. Let's do that," followed by the gentle voice of Edith.

"That sounds like such a good idea, Rosa. We'd love to join you. Where will we go?"

Before Rosa could answer, Jessica did.

"Number Seven is my room. We could go there. It has a ceiling fan."

Everyone smiled politely.

"Sounds good, Jessica. Lead the way."

Jessica's room was sunny and cheerful as the three women wandered about, sharing with each other the thoughts that came into their minds about what it would have been like to be a spinster or widow living here back at the turn of the century.

"I suppose they would have been a godly lot. Hymn books, lavender bags and lots of tea and fruit cake," commented Edith.

"Oh, how wonderful! Life was so simple in those days. I wish I was alive back then," said Jessica.

Rosa smiled at her companions.

"I just think of all the buttons – no zips – and whalebone corsets. And thinking of corsets reminds me why we're here."

Rosa walked over and stood beside the bed and lifted her dress over her head, folding it and placing it over the back of a chair. Then she kicked off her shoes and rolled onto the middle of the bed.

"Anyone going to join me?"

Jessica stared in amazement at her new older friend, lying back in just her panties and bra and shiny-black choker necklace and her red-painted toenails on tiny feet. Jessica thought how wonderfully relaxed Rosa seemed, and she immediately wanted to join her. And she wasn't alone. Aunt Edith was also looking intently at the reclining Rosa. Then she looked at her niece. Together they called out that they too were far too hot and that they would join Rosa on the bed.

Rosa was delighted, although confused at having to look at two women undressing on either side of the bed.

In moments Jessica had discarded her floral dress and sandals and she seemed unconcerned that she wasn't wearing a bra. She was probably used to not wearing one. It didn't occur to her whether or not it was inappropriate to join Rosa on the bed displaying her very flat little bosoms.

Edith had a lot more to remove, so it did take longer. She was aware that two sets of eyes were watching every garment being removed, but as items of clothing came off and she felt the gaze of her companions, she began to experience an anticipatory sensation which she admitted to herself, was strangely exciting.

When she at last peeled off her heavy tights, Edith felt less the conservative librarian and more the young adventurer, and when her clothing was reduced to just a bra and pants and she tentatively moved onto the bed and lay down beside Rosa, Edith was feeling like a very different woman.

"Welcome, fellow panty brigade members. Isn't this more comfortable? My best idea all day, I think. What do you think, Edith? Are you comfortable, dear lady, lying here in your undies?"

Jessica and Edith laughed. Edith stretched and spoke.

"I feel better than I have in years, Rosa. It gives meaning to that phrase I've never understood, 'Get your gear off.' It's better than a holiday, I reckon."

Jessica and Rosa laughed.

"Well, dear Aunty, I think it is great too. In fact, I think we should get our gear off more often."

Rosa mused about these two country women. She had liberated them this far, so how far could she take them?

"I hope we don't catch a cold. Some people's bodies are hotter than others' and it depends a bit on your body heat as to whether you start sneezing or not."

Rosa began to feel herself. First she put her hand on her belly, then she lifted a leg up high and pointed her toes, quite slowly and provocatively. She ran a hand down her thigh and reached under a leg to touch her calves. Then she felt her forehead and her neck just above her chest.

"I think I'm okay. I seem very warm."

Rosa's actions hadn't gone unnoticed.

"No, Rosa, I'm sorry but you've got it wrong. We can't check our own temperature. You can only tell how warm you are when someone else touches you. Like this!"

Edith reached across with a hand and placed it gently on Rosa's belly.

Rosa smiled with a look that indicated that she knew that what Edith had just said was not really true and was in fact an excuse for the woman to put her hand on Rosa.

"There you are darling, sorry, I mean Rosa. You feel quite cool to me, but what can you feel?"

Rosa laughed loudly.

"Actually, I think you are right, Edith. Your hand feels beautiful and warm. Does that mean I'm a bit cold?"

Rosa reached down and lifted Edith's hand and placed it on her own thigh, moving it just little as though she was being rubbed.

"Yes. You still feel warm, so I must be cooler. That is interesting. Can I touch you, Edith?"

Edith left her hand on Rosa's thigh.

"Yes, Rosa."

Edith reached over and picked up Rosa's hand and placed it on the top of her thigh.

"Oh Rosa! Your hand does feel hot."

Rosa and Jessica laughed.

"At the risk of sounding naughty, Edith, I think you touching me is making me hotter, but I do like it."

Rosa knew she was pushing things along a bit, but in just moments the woman's response was positive.

Edith laughed and said, "Well, I'm glad it's not just me, Rosa. Your hand is making me feel hotter by the minute and I don't just mean my body temperature."

Then Jessica called out.

"What about me? Is anybody going to make me hot? Would someone please give me a hand?"

More laughter and all the women moved their bodies, shaking off any residual defensive posturing that they might have carried.

"What do you think Rosa? Is Jessica a bit young for this sort of grown up activity? She's led a sheltered life, you know."

Rosa thought for a moment. These lovely ladies were responding in a way that could go anywhere or nowhere. But it didn't really matter. She was quite happy just lying on the bed in their delightful presence.

"Yes, maybe she is a bit young."

Jessica screamed in disbelief.

"Rubbish. I'll be twenty in a couple of months. Just for that, I'm having both hands, thank you!"

Jessica propped herself up, reached across Rosa, lifted Edith's spare hand and dragged it across and over Rosa, placing it low down on her belly. Then she lifted Rosa's spare hand and put it on her chest, just below a breast.

The two women adjusted themselves so that they could more comfortably reach Jessica. Both moved their hands just a little on Jessica, feeling the young woman's body.

Everyone was quiet for a full minute. Then Rosa dared to speak.

"Are we all feeling really hot now, girls, or is it just me? I'm feeling very kissy and kissable. Does anyone else fancy a kiss on their bare skin? No charge and no pressure; just asking."

There was a flurry of movement and both Jessica and Edith answered simultaneously.

"Yes, I'll have just a small one please," said Edith, in a hushed voice.

"Yes please, I think I'm old enough. Is that all right aunty?"

Laughter and then silence. Then Rosa warned, "Coming to get you. Edith, you're first."

She rolled on her side and stared at Edith who stared back defiantly. Then Rosa leant towards the woman and put her lips on Edith's and kept them there. Edith closed her eyes. Rosa then moved her hand from Edith's thigh to just below her neck and above her neat, well-formed breasts.

This was the moment of truth, thought Rosa. Would Edith respond or not?

Nothing was happening and Rosa considered it might be time to leave and go back to where they were before, but then something did happen.

Edith took her hand from Rosa's thigh and put it on top of Rosa's hand. Then she gently pushed the hand down to below her bra and carefully lifted four fingers from the hand and pushed them under the bra until they rested on a nipple. Then, as Rosa opened her mouth slightly to gasp, Edith put out her tongue and pushed it into Rosa's open mouth and they pushed their lips hard against each other. Both women sighed as Rosa fondled a stiff nipple beneath Edith's bra.

Rosa and Edith were now oblivious of the awestruck young woman watching their every move.

Edith's body became agitated and squirmed a little as she acknowledged her excitement, sensing that things had moved on.

Rosa couldn't take her mouth from Edith's, such was Edith's enthusiasm. Rosa surmised that this might well be the first real lovemaking that Edith had experienced in years. If that was the case, she would need a lot of it to satisfy her.

Rosa suddenly felt fingers moving up into her bra and a little voice behind her whispered, "What about me?"

Rosa didn't want to stop what she was doing with Edith. She figured that, as things were already moving fast, Jessica had absorbed the change in mood and was open to a sensual adventure.

Rosa moved her hand from Jessica's thigh, shifting it up just little so that it rested on the front of her panties. Then, with her index finger, she found her way around the panty crotch onto a little almost hairless patch. It was already wet. Rosa felt the girl stretching and opening her legs and she heard her groan.

Then Rosa took her hand from Edith's breast, found Edith's hand and slipped it down inside her own panties, showing Edith the way to her pussy, and after just a tiny hesitation to absorb this latest move Edith pushed at Rosa's mouth even harder while her tongue thrashed about trying to swallow Rosa entirely.

Edith's fingers were quick to react. Only moments after Rosa had put Edith's hand in her panties, her fingers began exploring Rosa's wet pussy, wandering everywhere, excitedly exploring this new wet and warm place.

Rosa thought about where they should go next. Everyone seemed happy, but things would need to change, even if only to rest their over-stretched arms. She decided that if she was right about Jessica's aunt, then Edith would go along with Rosa's plan. She took her mouth away from Edith's, looking at her lovingly.

"You are a very beautiful lover, Edith, but Jessica is feeling our love and wants to join in. Can I suggest that I change places with your niece? We have plenty of time and I will definitely want to kiss you again later. Just have a peep at Jessica and you will see what I mean."

Edith moved her head over to look past Rosa and saw Jessica lying with her eyes closed and Rosa's hand between her legs.

"Can I move her over here, Edith?"

"Oh yes, Rosa. Please do. I've so wanted to reach out to her lovingly for so long."

Rosa turned and spoke to Jessica.

"Jessica, darling. Edith and I want you to move over into the middle so that we can both make love to you. Is that okay?"

Jessica opened her eyes.

"Oh yes please, Rosa. And Rosa? Thank you. I love you so much."

When Jessica had moved over and settled back in between the two loving and very hot women, Rosa looked across at Edith and smiled.

"You start, Edith. Can I suggest kissing first? Everything is about kissing."

Edith smiled at Rosa.

"Thank you, Rosa."

Then Edith turned Jessica's face towards her and kissed the young woman, just as Rosa had kissed Edith, and Jessica groaned and pushed back hard on Edith's mouth.

Jessica quickly moved Edith's hand into her panties to continue where Rosa had left off.

Rosa watched with excited satisfaction as Edith removed her bra and pulled Jessica's face to her breasts.

Rosa congratulated herself, smiling with satisfaction as she contemplated the two near-naked bodies beside her, and listened to the sounds of lover's feasting on one another.

So where should Rosa go now? She already had tentative plans for these two, later in the evening, but for now she would content herself with licking and kissing Jessica's back and shoulders and touching her on any available spot without interrupting Edith in her loving efforts.

And being a woman with a voyeuristic bent, watching the two new lovers was divine and Rosa visualised those moments that, all being well, still lay ahead, when she would suck and lick both the women's pussies and watch their contorted faces as they came.

But things unexpectedly changed.

Rosa was suddenly jolted from her reverie when Edith screamed as she orgasmed and then burst into tears. Edith sobbed loudly, without any attempt to stem the flow of tears or the loud sobbing. She convulsed as she threw her body upward in a seemingly unending series of multiple orgasms.

Jessica stared at her aunt and then, instead of moving to console her, Jessica pushed Edith down onto the bed, holding her by the throat with one hand while dragging her legs apart with the other. Then she threw herself on top of her, thrusting hard against her groin and uttering incomprehensible sentences of violent love and passion.

Edith began to make a croaking attempt at speech which sounded like some multiple wave effect. Rosa could hear the two words she uttered constantly: "More! and Yes!"

In all the years that Rosa had enjoyed the company of lustful lovers she had never seen the likes of what she was now witnessing. Incredibly, Rosa, who was a master of control under any circumstance, found herself being drawn into this intense whirlpool of lust and release. Without a second thought, she found herself straddled atop Jessica's tiny bare thrusting buttocks and pushing herself against them in a frantic effort to share in this sexual explosion. She could just see Edith's red face over Jessica's shoulder. Jessica's hand was rigid around her aunt's neck and Edith's eyes bulged and rolled up and down.

Suddenly Jessica rolled over, pushing Rosa onto her back, and within moments the young woman was between Rosa's legs and thrusting like a wild animal. Jessica came, then Rosa came, and as Jessica fell over to the side Edith hoisted herself onto Rosa where she shagged her way to heaven, coming again with screams and tears and kisses and making Rosa scream her surrender to orgasmic paradise such as she had never experienced before and while the sex-crazed Jessica buried her face between her aunt's legs.

Three naked, exhausted and sheepish women stared at one another in silence. Then Jessica spoke.

"I'm going to come and live here in Sydney and you're coming with me, Aunty. And Rosa, we will want you to visit us. I want us to make love like this all the time. I adore you both."

Edith and then Rosa, kissed Jessica, affirming their willingness to all be lovers. Then Jessica pulled them both tightly to her and snuggled into them and sobbed uncontrollably.

2

WICKED AUNT

OVER A MOST ENJOYABLE Thai meal at their favourite restaurant, Edith and Jessica talked. They needed to sort out their relationship and this was the moment to do it. And it worked out well for both of them.

Edith's pending divorce and her desire to move to Sydney was central to the conversation and it benefitted both that she and Jessica establish early, and without rancour, that each would be better off living alone and independently. They would of course still be a loving couple but agreed in a remarkably frank manner that exclusivity was not a practical option and sharing their lives with others was both desirable and inevitable.

"There are just so many joyful options available to us, darling. So we should enjoy them while also enjoying each other," Edith said as she caressed Jessica's knee under the table.

"Rosa will have women scratching at my wicked aunt's door, I'm sure, not to mention Rosa regularly popping in to borrow a cup of sugar."

The two laughed openly about the possible erotic scenarios which might result from Edith's move into the Bennett's cottage.

Clearing the air was like a tonic and both women relaxed and happily held hands and touched each other. They hadn't been a couple for very long, only a few months in fact. But a lot had happened to them emotionally. Coming out as lovers and discovering a new world and ways of living and loving had changed them forever.

As the evening progressed, they even exposed their deeper thoughts and feelings, both freely admitting to feeling more assertive in the way that they wanted to experience their love life.

Edith told Jessica about their neighbour Roger and how she would like to know him better and how she had recently asked him to join her on a walk up the mountain. That triggered Jessica to ask when Edith would arrange for her to meet her new walking friend Chloe and Chloe's sister Lottie who Edith had told her about.

"It seems, dear aunt that you had a more exciting life in your monthly one week visits to Sydney than I do living here all of the time. I just don't seem to socialise enough. Maybe you could give me some tips now that you are a permanent independent woman around town."

Edith laughed and said she would. Then the two talked about all sorts of things. During the conversation, Edith said she had discovered that she was about to come into a little bit of money from an unexpected inheritance and that she would like to take Jessica shopping.

"I think its time you had a new wardrobe young lady. I'll transfer some money to your account this week It will be a birthday gift. You can then 'shop till you drop' as the saying goes."

"And does my wicked aunt have suggestions about what apparel this poor penniless student should adorn herself with? Would you like me in crotchless panties and see-through tops? Will I search for slutty shoes and alluring active wear? Will I dress up only for my lover or will I be flaunting myself and casting a wider net?"

Edith stared at Jessica with a bemused look.

"Hmm! Now that you mention it, you have matured noticeably in the past few months. I wonder if it's your sudden discovery of sex? Your bosom has definitely filled out and seems intent on making itself known to the world. It might even be large enough for an elegant little bra. Maybe we could start with lingerie. A set or two of sexy skimpy girly stuff. And a corselette would look nice on that super sexy little body. Your wicked aunt, not to mention most

WICKED AUNT | 13

of the rest of the world would find such things most easy on the eye."

The two were enjoying the banter and for once, Jessica wasn't hanging back when confronted with talk about the things that most women were interested in but which she had carefully avoided up until now.

Jessica's skinny body and lack of a bust had meant that she had hidden herself away from girly aspirations. Edith noted that this might be about to change. It also flagged the likelihood of the onset of an interest in boys and Edith was happy about that. She wanted the very best for Jessica and although relationships where fraught with possible difficulties, a woman's desire to have children was likely to come into Jessica's thinking eventually. Attracting a mate at the right time was important.

"We might start with the slutty shoes, darling. Although maybe they won't be too slutty. The sooner you get to practice walking in heels, the easier it will become."

Jessica let out a scream.

"You're really serious about this aren't you. You just want to make me into a bloody lipstick lesbian. I know where this is going."

Edith laughed and rolled her eyes, but Jessica was on a different roll.

"I will titillate you with the tiny lace thong panties with bows that I buy from Victoria's Secret, wicked aunty? And will I use their lip gloss or will a bright red old fashioned lipstick from the chemist do? Oh yes! We are going to have so much fun. I'll be a totally different woman after our shopping expedition. Is that what you want aunty?"

Edith leant forward with her arm under the table and pushed a hand up inside Jessica's shorts and let her fingers gently rub her lovers soft moist pussy. Jessica's draw dropped momentarily and she closed her eyes. Then, in a quiet voice said, "That is definitely cheating and I won't let you get away with it." Jessica slipped her hand up under her aunt's skirt and reciprocated. "Two can play that game, dearest aunt. Which reminds me, I want to talk about sex."

Edith sat with her eyes closed and her mouth slightly open then she refocused. "Yes, that is a good idea darling. I do too. You go first."

"No! You go first."

The two removed their hands and sat back.

"Anal sex is the subject of my talk today. Please listen carefully."

"Oh wicked aunt. You crack me up sometimes. Me thinks this might have something to do with what I saw in the carry-bag at home this morning. Very suspicious looking things from the sex shop. Is this what you are going to tell me about?"

"Yes I am! And didn't your mother teach you not to look into peoples shopping bags? Well, those things are butt plugs. You put them up your bum and wear them around the house or whatever, to stretch your anus for when you have anal sex later. I have been thinking about this for a little while and was going to gently introduce the subject at a proper moment. But now you know. I've wanted to try anal for a while now but didn't know how to bring up the subject. It wasn't until my new landlady, Rosa, gave me a tour which included seeing all of her sex toys, that my interest was reignited. So, there! End of story."

Jessica was suddenly the quiet little thing that Edith found so attractive.

"Oh Edith! I so love you. You know how I adore your bottom. I kiss it and lick it often as you know, and you always seem to enjoy it. Does this mean that we will be able to have each others bums as well as our pussies. Can we go home and start wearing the butt plugs now? Please auntie. Say yes. And I promise I'll go shopping if you come with me. I'll even buy heels and lipsticks. And if it makes you feel better, I'll ask doctor Meg to put me on the pill. You both want me on it, I know."

Edith burst out laughing. "You don't have to do anything you don't want to do darling. You know I love you just as you are."

Edith stood up and reached down and took Jessica's hand. "Come along darling. We have an urgent get-together with our derriere's at home. Lets not wait a minute longer."

3

MEMORIES

"Do you remember the Parker twins, Jess? It's a long time ago. I taught them at Sunday School."

It was early on a lazy Sunday afternoon and the two women were lying on the bed reading and happily enjoying their newly acquired butt plugs. Jessica turned and stared at Edith.

"Yes, I do Aunty. They left years ago and moved to Melbourne with their mother. Why do you ask?"

"Well, they've just enrolled here for elocution and singing classes. They will be living here until they find an apartment, according to Maude, so I expect we'll see them. They must be big lads by now. They were well built even back then, when they would have been around twelve or thirteen."

Jess continued to stare at her lover lying beside her in her bra and shorts. The two had just returned from a long walk in Eros Park.

"I didn't question her when she suggested she thought that the lads were bad boys these days. I wonder what she meant?"

The two went back to their magazines. Then Jessica rolled over to face Edith.

"Aunty, there is something I have to tell you about the twins. I want you to know and it's best I tell you now in case we suddenly meet up with them."

Edith rolled on her side to face Jessica and looked at her quizzically.

"You make it sound a bit ominous, darling. Tell me. And if I'm right you are blushing, which means that it is going to be embarrassing."

Jessica managed to laugh before launching into her story.

"I was eighteen and I was with my friend Prue, who was already nearly nineteen. It was the middle of university holidays. Prue had called at my place and we were heading over to her house to just muck about when we met the twins. They were at a loose end, so Prue invited them to come home with us. When we got to her house, she suggested we go out the back to the empty granny flat where we used to play around. Her gran had died a few years before. Prue's mother was at work.

The twins, Paul and James, would have been around eighteen and were easily influenced by Prue. Her breasts had also become noticeably larger since our school days. We both saw how the boys looked at them.

"When we got into the tiny cottage, the boys got decidedly amorous but after a bit of heavy petting we sent them on their way.

"I haven't seen the twins since that day because they moved away the following week which, when I think about it was probably a good thing, as was Prue leaving town with her mum a few weeks later."

Jessica stopped talking and looked at Edith.

"It's been so long that I've forgotten what they look like," muttered her aunt.

"Don't you remember Auntie? Paul was slightly taller than his brother and ..."

"No, darling. I mean cocks."

Jessica was wildly amused.

"Well, they were the only ones I've ever seen so that makes us about even, dear Aunt. I guess they would be bigger now."

"Do you mean the twins or their penises?"

Both women were enjoying their silly banter.

"I've told you as I thought you should know, aunty, in case we meet up with the twins, I'm pretty sure that when they see me their thoughts will go back to that day and if anything is said, I want to be sure you to understand what may be going on."

Jessica leant forward and kissed Edith. "I hope you are okay with that, Aunty. I've never mentioned it before. It seemed such a long time ago."

Edith put her arms around Jessica and pulled her close.

"You've made me really horny with that story, darling. I'm going to have you right now while thinking of holding and rubbing two happy cocks. What a lucky girl you were, and I'm already thinking we should ask the twins to come for afternoon tea. I'm more than happy to take off my knickers and let them spank their Sunday School teacher's bottom and taking anything else they might fancy, in return for a go at their willies. What about you, you cock-sucking little slut? Could you revisit those moments, darling? Could you manage the twins for an afternoon snack?"

Jessica had dragged off her knickers and was now removing her aunty's shorts and underwear, touching Edith's special places as she did so. Then in her pretend schoolgirl voice she replied.

"If you must invite the twin cocks for a visit, I will do whatever you want me to do and if it makes you happy I will entertain them in any way I can, one at a time or even both together if that would please you, dear wicked Aunty."

The two horny women laughed loudly and rolled around on the bed, grinding pussies together in a randy fit, thinking of stiff young cocks while kissing, licking and putting their fingers inside each other.

When the two lovingly lay back and regained their breath, Edith revisited Jessica's story.

"Darlene Higgins, your friend Prue's mum, had to leave town in a hurry because she got into a bit of trouble. You might remember that she was a physical education instructor at a private girls school.

"It appears that Darlene was reported to school authorities for interfering with a student, although it was said at the time that there was more than one involved. No charges were laid because the school wanted to avoid that sort of publicity. Darlene was advised to just disappear, and she did, to Sydney, I think."

There was silence as they lay thinking about what Edith had just said.

"I wonder if that had anything to do with Prue being the way she was."

"How do you mean, Jessica?"

"Well, it didn't really bother me but a couple of times when we were younger I heard people say that Prue was very mature for her age. I never thought much about it. She seemed like a good friend, but thinking back to that time with the twins makes me wonder what her relationship with her mother was really like. I guess we'll never know."

Edith looked thoughtful, pondering the situation.

"I should mention that, although our association was only to do with church and Sunday school functions, I found Darlene charming and very helpful. But we can never tell what people are really all about, can we darling? Life really does move in mysterious ways."

The two laughed, each thinking about her own situation.

"Now, Jessica. I'm thinking this would be the perfect time to take out our butt plugs and try using the small dildos. Are you up for it?"

"Oh yes, wicked Aunt. I would love that."

Edith turned the girl over onto her stomach and, with much giggling mixed with an occasional gasp, she removed Jessica's bright blue plug. Then she reached into the bedside drawer and took out a small dildo and a bottle of lubricant. While she was facing the drawer, Jessica asked Edith to be still for just a moment while she withdrew the black and silver plug occupying her aunt's large and shapely backside.

"Now it might take a few goes for this to be as good as we would like to think it will be. We will require patience, my love. The eight thousand nerve endings of the clitoris are spread all around, including around the lower side of the anus. Getting to enjoy some of those thousands might take a little practice, darling. Are you ready? Just tell me to stop if you are not comfortable."

Jessica moved up onto her knees and presented her backside to Edith.

"I'm ready, wicked Aunt."

Edith gently ran her hand over Jessica's sweet little bottom. Then she put two fingers into her anus, making an opening and squirted lubricant into it. Then she wiped lubricant onto the dildo and placed the end of it at the intended entry spot.

"Deep breath, darling. Here we come. Relax if you can."

Jessica mumbled a "ready Aunty" and Edith slowly pushed the dildo into the girl's bottom. Once the head was in, she stopped and watched how it was being received.

"Keep going, Aunty. All good so far!"

Edith moved the dildo slowly. It was sliding comfortably into Jessica without any difficulty. Edith stopped for a moment but Jessica said nothing. Edith eased the rubber thingy back a little, then forward again to see if there was any negative response, but there wasn't.

"Push it in further please, Aunty," were the only words Jessica whispered.

Edith pushed the dildo in, noting that it was in further than she thought. Three or four inches or more? Then Jessica moaned and whispered, "Move it backwards and forwards, Aunty. It's feeling really good so far."

Edith decided that there was no obvious cause for alarm and proceeded to gently shag Jessica's bottom, hoping the girl was going to be okay.

"Oh, Aunty, it's wonderful. I love it. I'm already feeling at least half of those eight thousand nerve endings. Push in a little further please."

Cautiously Edith pushed in, estimating there was now more than three-quarters of the rubber implement inside Jessica's bum.

"Oh, Aunty. It's so beautiful. I think I want to come already. How is that possible? I ... "

Before Jessica could finish she let out a mighty gasping hoot, first pushing back so that the dildo went all the way in, then arching her back and orgasming before collapsing on to her tummy, sobbing.

Edith gently rubbed Jessica's back and buttocks.

"Well, my beautiful girl. That was impressive. I'll leave our little friend there for you to take out when you're ready."

But Jessica had other ideas. She hadn't finished. She pushed back up onto her knees and instructed her lover to move the little thingy backward and forward again. Edith did as she was asked and Jessica came again, screaming as she did so.

Edith watched Jessica lying silent but with an occasional shudder. And when Edith gently touched her lover's buttocks, the girl screamed and came again.

4

DARLENE MEETS HER MATCH

It was a weekend when Edith had to visit her old home town and Jessica was alone in her little flat at 19 Eros Crescent. Jessica attended classes on week days and walked on the hill or went to movies at the weekends.

In hindsight, she might have remembered that old adage, "be careful what you think of because it might come true".

Returning from her walk in the bright sunlight and entering the dark hallway on her way to her room, a voice called her name.

"Jessica! Is that you darling?"

Jessica turned to see who it was, her eyes adjusting to the indoor gloom. What appeared to be a super attractive older woman was just closing the door of Maude's flat.

"It's me, Darlene; Prue's mother. You do remember me?"

Darlene stepped forward with her arms open and embraced Jessica before the girl could do or say another thing. The woman kissed her on the cheek before burying her face in the side of Jessica's neck, kissing her lovingly then whispered, "You haven't forgotten, you sweet girl, I can tell. There is so much to catch up on. Lets go in here. Maude is away until tomorrow evening. We won't be disturbed."

Everything was happening so quickly and Jessica hadn't had time to reason with herself about what she should do or say. As Darlene took her hand and led her through the door, Jessica's feelings whirled around and backward and forwards between alarm and sexual excitement. She didn't really know the woman, but what she knew made her uncertain of her situation.

When the two women were inside the flat, Darlene turned and put her arms around Jessica and smiled that same beautiful lipsticked smile and looked deep into the girls eyes.

Jessica's state of mind was becoming clearer and she realised that she wanted to know Darlene better, if only to discover more about her.

Jessica was older and her adventures with Rosa and Edith had given birth to a new sort of Jessica, one who knew what she wanted. Jessica's new more aggressive self came to the fore.

Without saying a word, Jessica eased a surprised Darlene down onto to Maude's big bed, her shapely shiny black stockinged legs and high heels hanging over the edge. Then Jessica lifted Darlene's skirt up far enough to see the tops of her legs and her black silk panties.

"I'm having you Darlene. I've heard a lot about you're earlier exploits. Now I'm the one in search of adventure and that includes your special spots, so just lay back. If you are good and do as you are told, I might let you have what you want, later. Are you okay with that darling?"

Darlene was in shock and her face was the picture of surprise. The sexy woman had always been in charge, had always taken the initiative, had always positioned the other person ready for her usual onslaught. Now she could only lay there, fascinated by what this thin and leggy attractive young woman was doing. Without thinking, Darlene found herself uttering her response in a soft little voice she never knew she had.

"Do anything you want to do to me you gorgeous sexy long-legged bitch. Anything at all! I so want to feel you Jessica. Do anything darling. I will love it. Hurt me if you want to."

Those last words rang bells in Jessica's head. She had discovered a reprint of an old book in Maude's extensive library in the common room and which probably shouldn't have been there. Jessica had found it fascinating. It was called The Pearl: A journal of Facetiae and Voluptuous Reading, first published in the late 1800s'. It was an early book of erotica and contained many stories involving disciplining of both women and men. Yes! She did want to discipline Darlene.

Through her recent reading, Jessica had discovered that there was an animal inside her that desperately wanted to express itself and now she had been given this opportunity, she would express herself to her complete satisfaction. The frustration she felt in not yet allowing herself to act the way she wanted to with her aunt, could now be expressed with the super voluptuous and sexual Darlene.

Edith had told Jessica how Maude had shown her around her flat, including opening the wardrobe door to let her see her sex toys and bondage collection, neatly displayed. Edith had mentioned seeing a little leather flagellator and other disciplining toys. Jessica took two steps back and turned and opened the wardrobe door and she saw everything she could possible want for this encounter with her willing older woman, now silently awaiting her fate on Maude's bed.

Jessica turned back to Darlene, lying back with her special place on view, albeit, covered by her sexy knickers. Jessica lent forward and slid the panties down over Darlene's shapely legs and threw them away. Then she fell onto her knees and pushed her head between the tops of Darlene's legs and when she had had her fill of Darlene's warm wet cunt, she told the resplendent woman to roll over onto her stomach and not move.

Jessica went to the wardrobe and selected a leather spanking paddle and spying an interesting looking strap-on dildo, she carried that back and put them both on top of the bedside cupboard. The hyper-horny young thing removed her own clothing then picked up the dildo and inspected it and licked the end before attaching it to her waist. Now Jessica was both armed and ready to fuck. Darlene lay silently ready and waiting, and breathing heavily.

When Jessica wrought her beast-like passions on the bare flesh of Darlene with the leather paddle, the sexy older woman cried out and shook her body and waved her stockinged legs and heels in the air but she did not call a halt to the things Jessica was doing to her. Then when Jessica pushed the freshly lubricated dildo hard into Darlene's vagina the woman simply screamed, "Oh yes you skinny bitch. Just give it to me!"

Such was the lustful passion felt and enjoyed by both women, Darlene suddenly saw clearly what she had previously avoided thinking about. Her love life had become jaded. So successfully did she hunt down her young prey, seduction had become too easy and predictable and she was now in need of something more. Unexpectedly, Jessica was giving her that something more she would never have guessed would be the ticket to a new world of anticipation and excitement.

Jessica heaved herself at the tangle of black wet curls between Darlene's legs, her mouth and hands working all the time. Sometimes she would stop and pull the big rubber thing out and stare at it and rub it, imagining she was a crazed lustful man. Then she would plunge it back into Darlene and yell and tell her she was a whore and a slut and that she was going to fuck her like this forever

Jessica grabbed Darlene's hand and pushed it between her own legs and made the woman rub her wet cunt, while she rubbed the woman's genitals and her large bottom.

After both women had screamed their orgasms and collapsed on the bed, there was silence only broken by the sound of Darlene sobbing as she lay quivering and shaking on the bed.

Jessica lay still. Her lover's rear remained a prisoner to their latest doggy position activities. Only occasionally did she move the dildo still firmly housed in her new sexy bitch-slave's cunt. Jessica took her in her arms, moving Darlene's face around and looking into her wet eyes and at her smudged lipstick lips and mascara streaked cheeks. Darlene was quiet but not yet finished, twitching and flinching and gasping and enjoying waves of tiny orgasms even as they talked. Darlene sobbed, reaching round and finding Jessica's pussy and clutched it tightly.

"I will want to fuck you like that again Darlene. Will you let me do it again?"

Darlene looked lovingly at Jessica.

"Oh yes, Jessica! And perhaps I can learn how to do it to you. In fact I'm going to buy sex toys immediately. It is time I caught up with the real world. Thank you for showing me, darling."

Jessica laughed at the thought.

"I suppose it's only right that you get the chance for a return match, you incredibly sexy bitch. Do you live far away?"

"Ten minutes on the bus at the most. If you promise me a repeat of today, I'll give you the address."

Jessica promised then said she had questions but only one was nagging her.

"What brings you to Maude's establishment, Darlene? Is Maude a lover?"

Darlene laughed out loud.

"Many years ago we ended up in the same bed while sharing and enjoying an exploit involving her neighbour and the woman's two teenage grand kids. I guess we've been friends ever since. We are not into each other but rather enjoy similar things.

"She contacted me recently to tell me there might be someone staying here that she knew I had known a long time ago. It piqued my interest and she invited me to call over and check them out. As it happens, I found you instead and that has been a wonderful surprise."

"So can I ask who the lucky person might be, if in fact you find them? Who knows? I might have designs on them myself and we will have to share them."

Darlene was amused but suddenly went quiet.

"Well, darling. We are talking about a long time ago."

"Like us, my love?"

"Yes, about the same time, probably. You may well know them. I know that my daughter had a moment with them. Do you remember Paul and James? Well, they are living here until they find an apartment. Now that they are grown up like you are young lady, I thought I'd casually call by and say hello. For old times sake."

Jessica screamed with delight.

"You are a sexy bitch. We've got them on our list. I've recently told my lover about the twins in case we are together when we bump into them and knowing that they might act strangely; if they even remember me of course. She got excited when I told her and we are now planning to have them for afternoon tea, so to speak. So there my love. It's a matter of who will get a hold of them first."

"Oh my God! Well, lets hope they are fit and well and have enough to go around. And I guess it will be first in first served."

The two women were now enjoying themselves with stimulating conversation instead of the stimulating of body parts and they were loving it. Then Darlene asked the question that had been running around in her mind for some time.

"So do I know your partner, Jess? From what you are saying, it sounds as though it is most likely a woman. Would I know her?"

Jessica suddenly realised that she hadn't once mentioned Edith.

"You do know her and you might be about to get a surprise, Darlene. She is my aunt Edith, until recently the wife of reverend John Campbell but now the ex-wife of the said sad gentleman. We've only been together a couple of months. At the moment she comes to stay here for a week each month but she's just taken a cottage a few doors up and will be moving in next week. There! Surprised?"

Darlene sat up with her mouth wide open.

"Oh my God! I remember her well. She was always so very nice to me. I thought how straight laced she was but liked her more because of it. In fact I thought she might just be hot but repressing it. I'm desperate to know how it all happened with you two but I guess we will have an opportunity to talk again. Now I will go home. I won't go looking for the twins tonight. It's unusual for me to say this but I think I'm satiated for the day, thanks to you.

"Can I meet up with Edith sometime darling? There is something about her which I find very attractive. I'd love it if you both wanted to have me for afternoon tea. Lets see? A jam roll together maybe?

"Now, before I leave. Will we just leave the twins as open game for whoever gets there first? They will probably be more fun on our own plus I think I'm greedy. Although if you do need any help with them, please feel free to call me."

Jessica looked at Darlene and burst out laughing.

"I should take a picture of you right now and upload it. I guarantee you would get a thousand likes and saves within minutes. You are the sexiest looking sex slave ever."

Darlene was sitting on the edge of the bed, her large shapely breasts and her neck were quite red and glowing. Her face was totally smeared with lipstick and mascara and her hair was in a crazy mess. She screamed and ran to the bathroom mirror where she screamed again and burst into laughter.

"Congratulations, darling. Never ever have I achieved this look. It just shows how good you are and how much I enjoyed myself. I would be more than happy if you gave me this look whenever you felt like it, Jessica."

The two tired women chatted while they dressed, enjoying conversations ranging from dress sizes to the price of deodorant. As they parted, they embraced saying how lucky it had been that they had rediscovered each other after all these years.

They swapped addresses and telephone numbers and Jessica said she would invite Darlene for a jam roll when Edith was next in town.

"Oh and Darlene?" called Jess from the front door, "I didn't ask about Prue?"

"A long story darling. I'll tell you next time I see you. Bye."

5

FROM RUSSIA WITH LOVE

IT WAS a long weekend and one when Edith was out of town.

Apart from Jessica, the house at number nineteen was deserted as far as she knew and she marvelled at the silence. Even the owner and music teacher, Maude, had left town and gone to Armidale to visit friends. She had offered to take Jessica with her but Jess was in no hurry to visit her old home town. Edith was there of course, but busy with preparations for leaving her job and friends.

Jessica stayed in bed for an hour longer than she would have on a week day when there were classes. She thought about this weekend and what she might do.

Looking out the window provided no clue about the weather because of the many trees that shaded this side of the building. If it was going to be a dull and cloudy day, she thought she would go and see a movie, maybe even two. And she would spend some time in the big bookshop close by. If it was a bright sunny day she would take a ferry on the harbour to one of her favourite spots and walk one of the beautiful bush tracks that would lead her to the next harbour ferry stop where she would hop on another ferry to another secluded harbour spot where she would find a cafe and have lunch.

Living in Sydney was a joy in every respect.

Stretching and moving her body felt nice and just for a moment, Jessica thought how good it would be if Edith were here and they could make love but she wasn't, so that was that. A movie or a ferry trip were the only things on offer. Then she heard the sound of a vacuum cleaner starting up in the passageway and realised that the cleaning ladies were there as they were every weekend. It might be holiday long weekend but the place still needed cleaning.

Meeting the cleaners when Jessica first arrived had been wonderful. The two well built Russian girls, Yula and Misha had laughingly pointed at her as she wandered down the hallway on her first day, fascinated with her long skinny body. They called out to her and asked her to tell them 'you name?' and when she told them, they argued intently with each other, Yula called out 'Sarai' while Misha shook her head from side to side and in a voice that signified finality, uttered 'Jeska'. Misha won the contest since they both now waved and called out Jeska when ever they saw her.

Jessica would dearly have loved to be able to have a conversation with the two women but it was near impossible.

The heavily Russian populated harbour-side suburb of Double Bay from where they came, along with the fact that they could easily get cleaning work meant that there was no great pressure on them to learn english. She guessed that they were somewhere in their early to mid thirties but it was hard to say. Being as large as they were made her think they were older only because Jessica imagined it would take some time to grow to that size, but then their youthful faces suggested a childlike naiveté and in the end Jessica remained confused about their ages.

A leisurely shower set the pace for the day and when she finished that, Jessica put her nighty back on and went to lay on the bed and read.

The sound of vacuuming was now quite close to her room but then it stopped and instead, she heard voices. First there was yelling and a loud woman's voice called out something in Russian.

While Jessica could not understand the words, the sound was one of surprise. Quickly, she rose from the bed and went to the door, but thinking there could be danger, instead of opening it, she peered through the glass of the little spy hole.

It was quite dark in the hallway but Jessica could just see a woman and a man standing and looking as though they were struggling or maybe holding onto each other while two more figures were rolling on the carpet.

Who should she call? Everyone was away and, not only that, she had left her phone on the piano in the music room back in the main part of house.

Jessica looked about, wondering what she should do. Then she saw the breakfast hatch in the wall beside the door. Now rarely used, this hatch was where the staff would leave a breakfast or lunch tray if the occupant had indicated they wanted to eat in their room rather than go to the dining hall. It was similar to the serving hatch still seen in many older motels.

The yelling had ceased but Jessica knew by the muffled sounds she was still hearing that something was happening. Quickly she knelt down and cautiously opened the sliding hatch door, making sure that the little chintz curtain covering the door was now behind her head to stop light from signalling her presence.

Suddenly she could see very clearly what was happening. Only a couple of metres across the hall in an empty carpeted alcove used for suitcases and luggage as people arrived and departed, Jessica could see two men standing in front of Yula and Misha. Each man had a hand holding the hair of the woman in front of them and each of the women had a cock thrusting backwards and forwards in their mouths.

Jessica scrutinised the faces of the men and quickly realised that this was the twins who she once knew, and yes, they were being bad boys.

Jessica had no knowledge of what led up to the scene she was watching. At first she assumed that the two ladies had been forcibly attacked, but first one then the other let go of a cock long enough to lift their dresses off over their heads and unclip and remove their brassieres to release their large breasts. Then they reached out and grasped and continued gulping on the twins penises. Jessica was forced to consider the possibility that this was not a rape situation but rather a mutual coming together.

The four figures continued their sexual adventure and Jessica began to feel aroused, putting her hand down between her legs, happily gazing at the scene in front of her. Large ladies happily slurping on large cocks was not something a girl saw every day. And looking at their breasts hanging and swaying backwards and forwards and side to side, Jessica found truly exciting.

Suddenly, Yula let go and swivelled round on her knees and thrust her giant bum in the air while yelling 'fuckie fuckie' and just as quickly Misha did the same and repeated the call 'fuckie fuckie'.

The twins dropped to their knees and as one, pulled down the knickers of each woman, each of whom reached back and divested themselves of the large garments.

A mass of hair, only partially visible to Jessica, confronted each twin as they held their cocks at the ready. Jessica couldn't quite see what the men were seeing, but she got the idea when first one then the other spat between the giant buttocks then planted themselves in where the anus was most likely the target, thrusting forwards whilst slapping the womens' backsides and yelling things which Jessica heard, but recognising only a couple of words, most commonly, 'fucking bitch'.

When the twins first pushed into the two women, Yula and Misha both screamed but after a few moments, they commenced a regular rocking motion suggesting that this was not something new to them. In fact, from where Jessica was situated she now saw that the two were holding hands and smiling at each other, unbeknown to their backend suitors. The two women moved rhythmically to the invading cocks and it wasn't long before the twins yelled and came.

Jessica watched, fascinated as the two men stood up and pulled themselves back into their trousers and then without even looking back at their willing partners, strode forward and out the front door, slamming it behind them.

The two huge and delightful naked women turned and sat back on the carpet then each reached out for the other and embraced and began kissing. Then each slipped a hand down between the other woman's legs, while the other hand cupped and lifted a breast to their mouth to lick and bite it.

Jessica was now rubbing herself quite energetically, but then she realised that there was something else she could do.

When Jessica opened her apartment door and stood in front of the naked ladies, the two looked at her and gasped.

"Jeska! Come Jeska," called Misha, in a rich soft Russian voice while gesturing with her hand.

Jessica went and stood in front of them and smiled and waited, knowing that they would want her. And they did.

Four gentle soft hands moved slowly up Jessica's legs sending the first shivers up her spine, then they reached further up under her nightie. She closed her eyes, happy to be the centre of their exploration. Then she lifted her nightie up over her head and suddenly she was naked and being drawn down to the carpet in between two adoring and sensual women. Never had Jessica felt so much soft flesh. First Yula had her way. She stretched a leg across Jessica's body and lay gently on top of her, feeding the young woman with a stiff nipple while she rubbed her cunt against Jessica's.

While she was doing this, Misha went behind her and began licking the crack of Yula's bottom and the sticky little orifice that had only recently been shagged by the twins.

Then the two women sat back and looked down at their long legged skinny sexy friend and smiled. Jessica lifted both arms and fondled each ones breasts causing them to giggle and wriggle their bodies with excitement.

Misha repeated what Yula had already enjoyed, staring down at Jessica with a loving smile as she shagged her. Jessica came again, just as she had for Yula, arching her back as the large Russian woman lifted herself up to allow her skinny girl to lift her body and scream her pleasure.

Then Jessica indicated that she wanted to bury her head between Yula's legs by pointing first to her own face and mouth and then Yula's mass of pubic hair. Not having the words, she gently pushed Yula backwards then turned herself around to offer her cunt to Yula's face while she explored Yula's sex. Yula happily obliged and parted her thighs. Her cunt was very hairy and very wet and the humid odour was very human and Jessica licked and loved and lost herself in this new and ever-giving and heavenly place.

While in this position, Misha moved around so that she could lick Jessica's bottom, slipping a finger in her little hole and slowly turning it in tiny circles.

Yula's mouth very quickly brought Jessica to orgasm and when that happened, both women groaned and shuddered in response.

After a little while, Yula removed Jessica's head and Misha took her place so that she could have another turn with their long skinny girl, and Jessica was in heaven once more and again orgasmed, screaming and repeating her Russian lovers words 'fuckie fuckie,' and 'yes', as she came.

As things slowed down, Yula and Misha took turns stretching Jessica across their thighs as if she were a baby, kissing her and pushing nipples into her mouth and gently fingering her pussy and sometimes her little anus. Jessica wanted to purr like a kitten thinking that these beautiful ladies were such a joy, and their feelings towards their baby Jeska appeared mutual. And she loved the sound of their voices, "Jeska like Misha's chast", which Jessica understood to be the Russian work for breast.

In the weeks ahead, and on the weekends when Jessica was alone, she would sometimes open her door when she knew that Yula and Misha were just finishing work and she would entice them in with a hand gesture and a smile.

She was excited at the idea of letting them play with the two dildo's that she and Edith had bought. And she was rewarded handsomely.

Fitting on the belts caused much hilarity and the happy ladies giggled and groped each other before shagging Jessica to orgasm and then each other. Then Jessica told them it was her turn and when she was at last let loose on the vaginas of the two incredible Russian ladies, kneeling on the floor with their rear ends wriggling and their buttocks flapping. Jessica went berserk until each one screamed and came, laughing and slapping her and each other.

This was truly a romp to remember and although Jessica eventually told Edith about everything that happened, by then Edith had moved to the cottage behind Rosa's house and Jessica's 'from Russia with Love' ladies were no longer working for Maud.

"Oh I'm so sorry I didn't get a chance to meet them Jessica. I did a couple of years of Russian at university. It would have been such fun. And so educational too, darling."

Jessica laughed at the irony in her aunts comment and prodded her in the ribs.

"I already know a little bit of Russian, dearest wicked aunty.

"Really, Jessica. I'm surprised. It's quite a difficult language. Tell me, sweet heart and I'll see if I know what you are saying."

Jessica stretched and sat up on all fours and pushed her bottom out provocatively towards Edith's face..

"Fuckie, fuckie, Jeska pliz, is all I know."

6

TWINS

IT WAS a quiet midweek evening when Jessica plucked up courage to go and knock on the door at the end of the corridor. Edith would be arriving on Saturday and Jessica hoped to organise an afternoon tea with the bad-boy twins. She wondered how they would react on seeing her for the first time after all these years. The thought caused a tiny quiver of excitement to run through her.

For just a moment when no one answered the door, Jessica thought there was no one home, but as she turned to leave the door opened a young man's head appeared.

"Hello. Can I help you?"

Jessica was surprised. This was not one of the twins. She watched as the door opened further and a second young man stood beside the first.

"Hello! I'm Damien and this is my brother Ashton. You live in Number 4, don't you? We've noticed you. What is your name?"

Jessica realised that things had changed and that the twins were not living here any longer.

"Hi Damien and hello Ashton. Pleased to meet you both. I'm Jessica, and yes I live down the hallway in Number 4. My Aunt Edith is coming down from the country. She's due here on Friday morning. I wondered if we could entice you in for afternoon tea on Saturday afternoon. A sort of welcoming party and a chance to get to know you both. Will you come?"

The two good-looking lads smiled at each other and nodded. Ashton, who Jessica thought might be the younger of the two, turned and smiled and answered, "We'd love to. What time would suit?"

"Let's say three o'clock? And by the way, what are you studying here?"

"We're both doing music theory and the history of classical composers. Only just started but I'm enjoying it and I think Ashton is too."

Damien looked at his brother then at Jessica.

"Yep! Love it so far."

"Okay then. See you both on Saturday afternoon. Thanks."

Edith's arrival was different this time. She had left her husband and her home. Her furniture and possessions were due to arrive at her new home behind the Bennett house at Number 1 Eros Crescent on Monday just after lunch.

Edith was excited to be in Sydney again and hugged Jessica, laughing happily about her new feeling of freedom.

When she had drunk her tea Jessica announced that she had been shopping as a result of their discussion during Edith's previous visit.

"Oh my God! What did you buy? Show me! Did you get the slutty stuff? Did you get the heels? I want to see everything."

Edith was unusually animated in her response to Jessica's announcement.

"Well, wicked Aunt. Seeing-as you seem genuinely excited, I just hope you won't be disappointed. Yes, I bought two pairs of high heels, the classic plain shiny black pair and a pair of red strappy sandals. And I bought lots of other little bits and pieces, which I will reveal to your appreciative gaze later. But first I must mention something that we are doing tomorrow."

Jessica told how she had gone to invite the twins for afternoon tea on Saturday, only to find that they had vacated their apartment and how she had been greeted by two nice young men who were brothers whose ages she guessed at around eighteen and nineteen. She told Edith that, not wanting to tell them that she was actually looking for the previous occupants, she had simply invited them to afternoon tea instead.

"They seem so young. Certainly not the bad boys we had hoped for, wicked Aunt. But they seem very nice and we'll all have fun, I'm sure."

Edith laughed and looked amused.

"Maybe it's an opportunity for you to dress up in your new clothes to get feedback from a younger audience, darling. Seeing a young man's reaction could be fun and it surely won't hurt them. In fact I could even wear my shortest skirt and stockings and modest heels and provide you with some competition. Who knows what turns young men on these days? An older woman's good legs might just play to their fantasies."

"You are truly a wicked Aunty and I'm grateful for that. But be warned that if things suddenly get exciting, it will become each slut for herself; suspenders and sharp heels and bras could become weapons, and may the winner take all."

When Edith, wearing her mature woman's outfit welcomed Damien and Ashton at the door and introduced herself, the boys stared at her, scanning her from her head to her feet. They seemed very surprised and smiled self-consciously at each other as though they were sharing a secret. And when Jessica called out her hello, the boys simply stared at her long legs, speechless.

Her attempts to look sophisticated and to walk normally in her new red shoes, caused her pelvis to sway from side to side. This exaggerated her already erotic persona so far as the two boys were concerned, even though she just felt clumsy and self-conscious. But when she noticed the effect her appearance had on the two young men, she relaxed into the moment, discovering the excitement of being the object of the male gaze. She had also noticed Edith's gentle smile of approval.

Chocolate cake and glasses of fruit punch made from white wine and lemon and ginger Kombucha fuelled a sense of revelry, with the boys telling stories of growing up in Queensland and attending a Christian Brothers school in Brisbane. But when Edith asked if they thought they would miss anything from their life at home, Damien and Ashton looked at each other then at Edith and smiled sadly.

"We do miss some things," said Damien.

"Special people," echoed his brother.

Edith maintained her loving, almost maternal smile.

"Who do you miss, boys? Your school chums? Girlfriends? Do tell us. Jessica and I would love to know."

The lads looked at each other as though they shared a secret.

"We can see by the looks you're giving each other that your missing your girlfriends, can't we, Jess?" said Edith, teasing them gently.

After a moment's silence Ashton spoke in a subdued voice.

"We're missing mum's friends Cynthia Chelsea. They come up from the country to stay at our place to keep an eye on us when Mum goes to Sydney to work for a week each month."

Edith saw that the boys were oddly self-conscious about their mothers friends in a way that suggested some deeper feelings. Edith noted that, during afternoon tea, the younger lad had twice said the name Chelsea when he addressed Jessica and then rushed to correct himself. Something about Jess certainly resonated with his memories of his cousin.

The young men had settled comfortably on the settee with tummies full of sausage rolls and cake and fruit punch, enjoying the female company, and both were happy to converse on any topic that was raised. When Jessica and Edith asked questions about girlfriends, instead of colouring up and mumbling, the boys laughed and looked at each other and without thinking Ashton blurted out that they didn't need girlfriends.

Edith thought about what he had said, then took a punt and asked a question.

"So, you two are obviously close to your mum's friends. Are they affectionate and loving women? Do you go out together or do fun things together?"

The slightly tipsy lads smirked at each other and Damien giggled, "They like to play with us."

Edith and Jessica were intrigued and exchanged glances. Jessica responded quickly, "What sort of games do they play with you Damien? Sounds like it could be fun."

Whether it was Jessica's endearing looks and soft appealing voice or her long stockinged legs or the alcohol in the fruit punch the two women never knew, but when Damien announced without hesitation, "They make us take our trousers off," Edith and Jessica gasped and his younger brother uttered a loud "Yes!"

The two women exchanged meaningful looks and nodded to each other.

"Do your lady visitors remove any of their clothing?" Edith asked in a quiet and matter-of-fact voice.

"Yes, they take of their skirts and tops."

"And then what do they do, Damien?"

"They tell us that we cannot do anything other than what they tell us to do. Then they hold our cocks and put them in their mouths."

"And do you both like having your cocks in their mouths, boys?"

"Oh yes, we love it. That's what we're missing most."

Edith and Jessica looked at each other and smiled, then Jessica volunteered a suggestion.

"Edith, I'd like to help Damien and Ashton get over their sense of loss, wouldn't you?"

The two lads watched as Edith reached out and took Jessica in her arms and kissed her passionately, letting one hand slide over Jessica's breast and sliding the other hand up under her dress. Jessica pushed her legs wide apart and stared into her lover's eyes. It was a spontaneous show for their young visitors, staged to let them know that their hosts were into the loving things that some people enjoyed. Then both turned and stared at the boys.

"We want to help you both get over missing your lady friends Cynthia and Chelsea. Jessica and I would love to be your pretend lady friends while you are here in Sydney. Take off your trousers right now and we'll take off our skirts and tops and carry on from where Cynthia and Chelsea left off. Let's do it right now, boys?"

It took only moments for Edith's offer to register. Both boys speedily dropped their trousers to the floor. Then they watched dumb-founded as Jessica stood up and lifted her dress up over her head and dropped it onto a chair while Edith unzipped her skirt and stepped out of it and then removed her blouse.

What a sight it was for two young hormonally charged men. Edith in her cream-coloured corselet and with her suspenders reaching down over the tops of her bare legs to hold up her tan stockings. And Jessica's amazing long skinny legs in girly white stockings with lacy thigh-hugging elasticised frills around the tops and her tiny knickers and matching red bra.

"Now, boys, the rules are the same as Cynthia's. No touching us unless we tell you what we want. Okay? And it's okay for you to call me Cynthia and Jessica probably won't mind if you call her Chelsea. Is that okay with you, Jessica? Now, are we ready?"

Edith reached forward and pulled down and removed Damien's underpants and Jessica immediately repeated the action with Ashton. Two rapidly rising pink cocks greeted them and the two women looked hungrily at them and each reached forward and grasped one. Each held one gently in her hand, turning and smiling at the other.

"It's so nice that we can help these boys out in their hour of need isn't it, Jessica?"

But Jessica couldn't reply. She had already placed the head of Ashton's cock in her mouth and was gently running her tongue around its head. Edith looked at the beautiful Jessica kneeling on the carpet in her skimpy underwear holding a cock in her hand and mouth and with her eyes closed, delighted that her lover was enjoying a man for a change. Edith did the same to Damien and the two young men watched through glazed eyes.

The two women, with cocks in their mouths and savouring the soft but firm flesh of healthy penises were in no hurry to move on. Such delicious moments were to be savoured. But then Edith, thinking of her responsibilities – as she chose to regard them – looked up at the two happy lads and spoke. She continued holding Damien's cock with one hand while gently caressing his scrotum with the other.

"At some time in the not too distant future, when you are with a girlfriend in this situation, you need to remember that for her to be happy, things need to move slowly, at least in the beginning. Once she has your cock in her hand, let her set the pace so that she gets to enjoy it. If you do that, you will be well rewarded by her enthusiasm for what you both do later. If you always put your girlfriend first, you will enjoy the best of times."

Edith fed the now rigid cock back into her mouth and continued savouring the moment, realising that she was enjoying something she had long since given up thinking she would ever experience again. Having this situation suddenly happening to her was another milestone in her move towards freedom. She had not handled a man in this way in more than fourteen years and nerve endings all over her body responded in a way she no longer thought possible.

Jessica slipped a hand across and caressed Edith's leg just above her stocking, taking Ashton's cock out long enough to murmur to her lover, "I'm loving this, darling. I think I just want to suck cocks forever."

Edith smiled as Jessica slipped him back into her mouth, her fingers now touching and rubbing the young man's testicles. "I think you are going to get as much as you want from now on, darling. Now, just for fun, shall we swap?"

The two women looked up and smiled at the Ashton and Damien, then they swapped places. Each took a new cock into her mouth and continued as before.

"You lads might like to feel our titties. Jessica and I are just removing our bras. Now the important thing with breasts is to be gentle with them. Rarely, if ever, does a woman appreciate being mauled with groping hands. If you have groping inclinations, which is natural in most men and many women, then learn to grope gently and probably a girl's bottom is a good place to start. You could occasionally nip a nipple between thumb and finger or playfully stretch them gently away from her breast, but the general rule must always to be gentle."

Jessica had listened to her aunt's wise instructions and had quickly removed her bra, exposing her small but cute rounded breasts and Damien was already there with a hand cupping each one. Edith had removed her bra and her adequate breasts were now being lifted and fondled enthusiastically by the young Ashton.

After a good ten minutes of cock-sucking and breast-fondling, Edith figured she should offer the young men the next moment of enjoyment. She knew that, however much girls liked sucking, it could become boring for a man if it went on for too long, given that most men were generally desperate to move to the next moment of excitement.

Edith touched Jessica so that she stopped sucking and looked up at her aunt. Edith pointed to her mouth and puckered up and Jessica obeyed, leaning over for a kiss. Then Edith whispered her instructions.

"I think we should let the boys come soon. Are you happy to get vigorous, darling? When he is ready to come, aim him at your mouth or your breasts, or you can suck him off in the final moments if you prefer. Please yourself. Oh yes, and look lovingly up at his face and make eye contact if possible. It makes a difference. Oh, and Jess? I think we should let them go a little further with us next week maybe. Think about it. We can talk about what we'd like later."

Jessica smiled and went back to Damien's cock. She made slurping noises just for the fun of it as she dragged him into her mouth as far as she could.

"Now lads, we think its time you both came. Cynthia and Chelsea will masturbate you and you can come in our mouths or on our breasts or our bellies. Whatever! Ready?"

The two women began to handle the cocks with a much tighter grip and faster movement and it wasn't long before both boys groaned and yelled.

When the moment came for her cock to explode, Jessica pulled Damien right into her mouth and wouldn't let him go as he spurted his copious offering down her throat. Edith spread the young Ashton's amazing torrent all over her breasts as she beamed a beautiful smile up at his glazed eyes.

Four bodies lay about the floor. Jessica rubbed her pussy and licked cum from her aunt's chest while sharing her with Ashton, who was obsessed with Edith's large stiff and beckoning nipples. All four were at peace with the world.

"Well, I think we all enjoyed that. Will you boys make yourselves available next Saturday? If you are, get yourselves scrubbed up and over here at let's say, six-thirty. We'll order in a pizza."

"We will definitely be here Edith, that's for sure. Oh my God! Quick Ashton! Mum's ringing on the landline in our flat at 8 pm. We've gotta go. Thanks, Jessica and Edith. That was fantastic. Just what we needed."

In moments the two lads had gone and Edith and Jessica closed the door and then collapsed onto the bed.

"Yes, it was just what we needed wasn't it, my dearest wicked love."

"Yes, you sexy cock-sucking slut, but now I need you to suck me."

Within moments they were both rolling and kissing and biting each other on the bed.

"I don't want to be groped gently, my love. I want you to tear me to pieces and eat me all up."

Edith had asked Jessica earlier for ideas about what they should do with their neighbours this time. Last week they had sucked the boys' cocks and made them come.

"Well, wicked woman, I will be guided by you. Personally, I just love sucking their cocks. In fact now that I think about it, when I grow up I wouldn't mind becoming a professional cock-sucker."

Edith giggled and slipped a hand up Jessica's skirt.

"Not wanting to rain on your parade, darling, but may I suggest you complete your music studies as planned? I'm sure you will find time to follow both passions. The world is not going to run out of cocks any time soon. Just take your time and you can have all of them."

Jessica smiled and said she hoped that was true.

Damien and Ashton arrived at exactly six-thirty the following Saturday. Both were eager for their next session and lesson with Jessica and Edith. The two women welcomed them with glasses of fruit punch, and when the pizza was delivered just moments later, they all sat and enjoyed a meal together.

"Well, boys, are you ready for a little bit of learning fun? We hope you are. Jessica and I have a new activity for you which we feel sure you will enjoy. So come and stand in front of us and take off your pants. We'll start with a sucking session just to warm us all up."

Edith and Jessica made themselves comfortable on the settee while the boys divested themselves of their trousers and underpants. Then they stood in front of the two women with their rapidly rising cocks waving happily in anticipation of what was about to happen to them.

Jessica was in such a hurry to get Ashton into her mouth that she forgot to open her blouse. Then she saw Edith removing her top and undoing her bra so she followed suit, managing to do the same without letting go of him.

Jessica revelled in what she was doing, sometimes holding Damien's penis in her hand while she licked it up and down and over the hood. Then she would pop him back in and slide him deep into her throat, vividly recalling the week before when he had shot his bolt down her throat. All the time she made slurping and sucking noises. Occasionally she would pop her head down lower and kiss and lick his balls, before returning to the main course.

Next to her, Edith was happily sliding Ashton's member around in her mouth and licking him and fingering the slippery-looking head so that he trembled and breathed deeply.

After a little while the two women moved the boys, making them swap places so that each could try the other.

"Now boys, this week we are going to put your cocks in our pussies, or perhaps we should call them our vaginas. But before we do this we must do one important thing. We live at a time, unfortunately, when it is not uncommon to catch some sort of unpleasant complaint from having unprotected sex, even if it is with someone who you know very well. So what should we do?

"Wear a rubber?"

"Well, done, Ashton. Yes, we must wear a condom. So I have them here and Jessica and I will put them on for you. Secondly, you may well tell your girlfriend that you will not come in her pussy, but she should still not allow you in unless you are wearing a condom.

The other thing worth remembering is that, if a younger woman is in love with you, it is possible – though it rarely happens – that she will tell you that she is on the contraceptive pill when she isn't. This is called entrapment: when a woman traps a man by getting pregnant to him."

There were a few giggles and comments as Jessica and Edith rolled a condom onto each boy's penis. Then they ran their hands up and down the newly dressed dicks to "iron out the wrinkles" as Edith laughingly commented.

"Now, boys, before we pop you in, you need to know that whoever you are popping it into will want to feel ready; and ready means, among other things, wet or lubricated. Never try to enter a dry vagina, for both her sake and yours. There is a lubricating gel that is easily bought at the chemist if you need it. Now, are you both ready?"

The boys nodded enthusiastically and stared as they took off their skirts and pulled down their knickers and threw them onto a chair across the room.

"Now there are two main positions that people like for having sex, missionary position and the doggy position. We will start you off with the missionary position. We will lie down with our legs apart and you two should position yourselves by kneeling between our legs."

Jessica lay back on the carpet, her long legs opened out in a welcoming fashion. Then Edith did the same and the two bent their legs at the knees and asked the boys to bring their cocks up close to the bushy places in front of them.

Then both women reached out and each drew a cock up to the entrance of her vagina and with a little bit of rubbing up and down slid the boys in.

"There, boys. Well done! Now push your cocks in as far as you can. We will tell you if there's anything wrong."

Jessica was lying with her eyes closed. This was the first real cock she had ever had inside her. Many times Edith had taken her with a dildo, but now this was the real thing and she hoped it would be as good.

"Now boys, you can do whatever you would like to do now. Gentle is always good, but we won't mind if you get vigorous. And whenever your ready, ask us to roll over to show you the doggy position."

The boys took control and shagged away in the women's special places. Then first Ashton and then Damien asked for each woman to roll over and get up on her knees, and the two discovered the wonders of the doggy position and the excitement of being able to look down on that other interesting place nestled between the buttocks.

When the boys had left and gone across the hallway to their own unit, Jessica and Edith flopped onto the bed and sighed.

"Well, wicked Aunty. I enjoyed that boy thingy. He managed to come at long last. I enjoyed that moment the most. Really cool! I guess they will get the hang of things as they go along."

"Yes, darling. I'd quite forgotten that it was your first real dick. So glad it worked out for you. Did you notice the difference?"

"Well, Edith my dearest. So much depends on who's doing things and what they are feeling, I guess. You are a wiz on the rubber cock and so I'm spoilt, I suppose. Having feelings for someone or feeling that someone is really into you and that you have excited them, would obviously decide how things work out. I suspect that what we had tonight was a bit clinical. I certainly wasn't carried away. And I think that the boys were so busy working things out that they didn't manage to get emotionally involved in any way either. Never mind. Now if you've got the energy, wicked Aunty, put Rupert Rubber on and give it to me like it matters. Fuck me please, Edith. I'll do anything you want."

It wasn't long before Edith had strapped Rupert on and was straddling Jessica, who reached her legs high into the air and screamed. "Yes, please you wicked woman! Don't stop!"

7

CHLOE

THE TWO PEOPLE that were originally going to be living together but in the end chose not too, were Edith and Jessica. But living at different ends of the same street meant that they would not need to forego their times together. And they, like Maude and the others living in number nineteen, had each other for company if and whenever they wanted.

Edith and Jessica had the boys on hand and could also still get a pizza delivered, although it sometimes took a little longer.

But then they learnt that they would now be sharing the boys with the very sexually active Maude and possibly with the two new girls who moved in to number eleven just before the lock down. Jessica and Edith's plans to invite the new girls in for a pizza, were in hand.

Edith still went for her walk on Mount Eros on most mornings where she usually met her friend and neighbour, Chloe and the two, more than not, would spend loving time together in Chloe's secret cave.

It was thanks to the Corona virus lockdown, that Jessica met Chloe. Edith had long wanted the two to meet so when Jessica was unable to attend classes, she accompanied Edith on her walks.

Jessica and Chloe were instantly friends. Both knew that the other understood Chloe's relationship with Edith. And when the rain fortuitously arrived on their first walk together, all three made haste to the hidden cave and it was only a few minutes before Jessica had Chloe underneath her on the carpet of leaves with Edith dragging first Jessica's then Chloe's shorts and panties off before sitting beside them with her bare breasts available for the occasional grope from both girls and quietly touching each ones special places.

8

BIRTHDAY SURPRISE

DARLENE HAD ALREADY CAUGHT up with Edith some weeks earlier, when Jessica had arranged afternoon tea so that the two could meet up again after a gap of more than seven years.

The meeting had been memorable for the loving way the two eventually kissed and fingered each other and excitedly made love, inviting Jessica to join them.

A wonderful conversation ensued about their lives in Armidale about so many people, some who Jessica knew and other she'd had never heard of. There was sadness and scandal and gossip and the two older women confessed that it had been wonderful catching up and seeing each other again after all those years and how it had been most cathartic.

"So lets invite Darlene over for her birthday, Edith announced one evening. It's the weekend after this. Are you happy with that Jess?"

"Sure, Edith, she's such good fun and her more than adequate sexy body offers so much to touch and play with, and you two already act like you are old friends. Yes, call her now, wicked aunt, before she gets a better offer.

Darlene answered, "Yes please, I would love that."

"Great! Lets get a Thai takeaway and I'll make a birthday cake. I won best cake twice in high school so trust me aunty."

All was settled but when the two were reading in bed later, Edith suddenly said, "I think I'll plan something a bit special for her birthday, Jess. Let me tell you and you can tell me what you think."

———

Jessica's birthday cake was a great success and Darlene and Edith had second helpings. Darlene looked sexy as she always managed to do. It was partly what was going on inside her mind, Jessica mused as she blatantly stared at the woman's legs and shoes and her tight skirt and tight blouse. It seemed every part of Darlene was available for sensual adventures, especially her willing attitude.

After dinner Edith dimmed the lights and she and Darlene settled on the sofa, while Jessica cleared away the food and dishes. When Darlene offered to help Jess answered with a slight mocking tone.

"It's your birthday celebration, Darlene. Sit back and Edith will look after your every need. In fact I think she's planning something special. Is that right, darling?"

Darlene beamed and her big bright red lips opened as she laughed and replied. "Just so long as it involves being touched, I will welcome anything on offer. You know that I'm just a slut. So what am I about to get, Edith my darling."

There was suddenly a knock on the door. Edith called out to Jessica in the kitchen.

"I think there is a delivery at the door, Jessica. Would you get it please."

Edith went back to what she was about to do which was to slide a hand up under Darlene's skirt.

"Who is it, darling?"

"It's our neighbours, Edith. They want to wish our visitor a happy birthday and to say goodnight."

"Bring them in. I'm sure Darlene would love to meet them."

With that, Jessica came in leading two slightly embarrassed young men in their pyjamas. Damian and Ashton stared at Darlene in all her sexy finery like she was a gift from heaven. Then they walked over and stood in front of her and Darlene stared in amazement as the lads pulled their semi erect cocks from the fly in their PJ's and pointed them at her. Then in awkward voices, they managed to sing the first few lines of Happy Birthday.

"Boys? This is our very good friend, Darlene. Darlene, these lovely young men are our neighbours, Ashton and Damian. They are often visiting us on a Saturday night when Jessica and I read them bedtime stories."

Jessica watched as the super sexy woman first looked at Edith and then, smiling with her radiant sexy smile, reached out with both hands and grasped a cock in each.

"Oh my God, this is the most amazing present ever. So please to meet you Ashton and Damian. Am I allowed to suck you?"

The boys murmured their consent. Then Ashton asked Darlene if she would mind if they touched her breasts.

"I would love you to touch me anywhere you feel like touching. Edith and Jessica will both tell you how I love to be touched. Do whatever you want. Will it help if I take off my skirt?"

Damian nodded and said it would help a lot and in no time at all, Darlene's substantial stockinged legs were available as were here beautiful tits.

Darlene drew the two cocks to her and began to suck them. Then she looked at Edith who was happily staring at what was going on beside her.

"Darling, help me with one of these please, at least until I get going, then I might want it back."

Edith moved up closer to Darlene and willingly took one of the boys in hand.

Jessica had no intention of returning to the kitchen while this super hot scene was happening in front of her. Instead, she plonked herself on the arm chair opposite and removed her panties and began to play with herself while watching the boys four hands exploring Darlene's super body and Darlene and Edith's heads moving backwards and forwards. She admired Darlene's large red lips and her outstanding nipples.

Darlene uttered noises of satisfaction and excitement and she slid herself downwards and opened her legs wide showing that she didn't wear panties and that all that a man or woman could want was available at the top of her large stockinged legs.

Edith's lad retrieved his cock, politely muttering, "Excuse me for a moment please." Then he buried his head between Darlene's legs to explore her cunt with his mouth.

Edith took the opportunity to lean in and whisper to Darlene that she and Jessica had only last week, taught the boys why and how they should use condoms. She said she's mentioning it just so that Darlene can reassure them that it's okay not to if she's okay with it and wants them to shag her.

Darlene smiled lovingly at Edith and mouthed the words "Thank you."

The sucking and licking and groping went on for some time and then Darlene announced in a quiet voice.

"I would love you both to put your cocks in my pussy. It's okay. You won't need a condom."

The lads wrestled briefly for first position.

Ashton was invited to be first and was guided into Darlene's wet cunt. She lifted her legs up and they hung in the air like waving flags of celebration as the lad pushed into her. Only moments later, he came along with a lot of verbal utterances, and then as he withdrew his brother presented himself to the beautiful smiling woman who quickly slipped him in to a very slippery heavens gate and very soon, he too was relieved of his load.

Not long after, and each carrying a plate of cakes, the boys said their farewells and headed out the door.

Jessica immediately moved over to the settee and pushed her face in between Darlene's legs, intent on licking up what the boys had left behind, sucking and swallowing their cum with gusto.

"Wilful waste makes woeful want." Jessica whispered, licking her lips with a satisfied smile.

Edith looked at Jessica quizzically. "Should I worry about this girl, Darlene?"

"Well, darling, we all think a hearty appetite is a good thing, don't we. From more cocks than I can ever remember, I've guzzled a lot of it and I've always found it to be good for my complexion. No wrinkles yet."

Darlene lay on the settee in a languid state of undress, one hand fingering a breast and the other between her legs rubbing her newly saturated pussy and smiling as Jessica brought out coffee and the remains of the cake.

"I don't know how to thank you sexy bitches for that wonderful birthday present. It was truly awesome. Who would have believed it could have happened just like that."

"Well, Darlene. Just so long as you are happy for us both to molest you on a regular basis, then no thanks is necessary. But we are both very glad you enjoyed it. We were a bit nervous when we first thought about it but then we just said, what the hell."

The three enjoyed their coffee and cake and talked about various things. But then Darlene looked across at Jessica.

"I keep forgetting to tell you, Jessica. Prue has said on the phone, how much she would like to see you. She lives with my mad sister Annabella and her husband Brendan on their sheep property thirty kilometres west of Goulburn."

"I should tell you that Prudence got into a mess in her late teens. She started living with a drug dealer and had only just started using heroin when the man was arrested and sent to jail. She was cautioned and had counselling and fortunately, being essentially a sensible woman, she saw how important it was for her to get away from Sydney.

"She's been living on the farm with Bella and Bren for over two years now and she loves it. And she has made a lot of friends there, too.

"Anyway, I was thinking that with holidays coming up and me due for a visit, you might like to consider coming with me and although I'll only stay a couple of days, you would be very welcome to stay longer. When you are ready to come back, there is an evening bus from Goulburn that gets to Sydney around eight o'clock. What do you think? And Edith, what are your thoughts?"

Edith answered first.

"Well, I was only thinking about the school holidays yesterday. My solicitor wants me to go back to Armidale for a few days to make an inventory of my stuff and I want to arrange for a carrier to bring some of the stuff to Sydney. I hadn't mentioned it to Jess as yet as I was waiting to get more details from the solicitor before committing to a date. May I suggest that a trip to Goulburn might be a better idea than an as yet unconfirmed trip to Armidale? But what do you want to do Jess?"

Jess looked at each in turn and smiled.

"Hmm! Rarely does a gal get this much choice. I had planned a shopping trip to New York or maybe Paris but now I think about it, counting sheep in Goulburn sounds far more exciting, even better than counting knives and forks and spoons in Armidale. I'll go with the sheep option if that is okay with you Edith. But if you need me to come with you, just say."

"No, sweetheart, I'd prefer you went with the sheep option to be honest. I can't guarantee that there won't be hostilities with the ex while I'm up in Armidale. And you definitely don't need that.

It was decided there and then that Jessica would travel with Darlene in a fortnights time.

"I suppose I should get dressed and move my lazy self," Darlene announced.

Everyone agreed that the birthday party had been a cock-up in the most splendid way, and the ladies ended their night with kisses and touchy goodbyes.

SPRING IN THE AIR

Darlene collected Jessica mid morning for their trip to Goulburn. It was a beautiful early spring day and they both rejoiced that they were leaving the city and going on an adventure.

Jessica was intrigued by Darlene's move into a spring time wardrobe, a relaxed floral dress and low sandals and a linen jacket was about it although there was obviously a large bra beneath the dress. Her deep cleavage and shapely arse were the only signs of her innate sexuality.

"Well, Jessica. I hope you are ready for a country style adventure."

Jessica thought for a moment then wondered what sort of adventure Darlene was referring to.

"You make it sound slightly mysterious, Darlene. Is there anything I should know about before we get there?"

They had just left the Western Freeway and were heading directly west towards Goulburn.

Darlene gave a low chuckle.

"Muta East Station is a very large sheep and grain property of around sixty-thousand hectares. As well as that, Brendon and Annabella along with Brendan's brother Gary, own a second even bigger place over near Cobar where the country is drier. There they run mainly cattle. This means that they have a very large permanent staff. Add to that the contractors who come and go; shearers, shed hands and harvesting contractors, etcetera. All in all, there are always at least fifty or sixty people at Muta East at any time. It is like a small village."

Jessica was impressed. She had never suspected that farms could ever be that large.

"So I guess they are just men there, or are there woman farm workers too?"

"Oh there are plenty of girls. There are women who work in the shearing sheds sorting fleeces and stuff, there are women who work in the kitchens and help maintain the living quarters and tourist accomodation, and there are Jillaroos as well as Jackaroos although they are mainly at Cobar, at Muta West.

"But I guess I should tell you a few other important things before you get there, Jess, just so you won't get too shocked or confused. Because I know everyone and have visited over the years, I've grown accustomed to, shall we say, the eccentricities of the locals.

"Out in the country, people have to make their own entertainment. Even though they now have satellite TV and Netflix, they still need to interact with one another or at least tolerate each other. The significant thing about country folk is that they tend to be more accepting of odd behaviours and even start to see some of them as normal, simply accepting people for who they are, not what they should be."

Jessica stared at Darlene. She noted that the woman still wore the bright red lipstick she wore when she was dressed in her seductive city evening wear.

"Well, Darlene. You've got me interested. What strange behaviours will I need to watch out for. Sounds quite exciting. Please tell."

Darlene was busy thinking about what to tell Jessica and what not to tell. Somethings could be left for her to just find out about on her own, probably after Darlene had left.

"Well, Jessica. You've obviously noticed what I am like and how I am what some people would label highly sexed, or in the old language, a nymphomaniac."

Jessica interrupted, laughingly saying that she really hadn't noticed but now that Darlene had mentioned it, she did recall moments when she had observed certain exciting behaviours.

"So, I'm forty-nine and my sister Annabella is forty-seven. If I tell you that Bella is at least twice as sexually active as me and, some would say, totally mad, would you therefore assume that my sister could lead a very interesting life?"

"Wow! I certainly would, Darlene. But if she lives out of town and helps her husband run the property, how does she manage to have two separate lives? I mean you, her big sister, doesn't have to consider a husband when planning your fun, do you? So how can she manage affairs and such?"

"The clue to all of it is that Brendan accepts her for who she is. Not only does he accept her, he encourages her to do anything she wants. We're talking sexual things here. In fact Brendan enjoys watching Bella with another man and sometimes with more than one man. He's not gay or bisexual, just very happily in love with her and accepting of whatever she does."

Jessica sat staring at the woman, her mouth open in obvious amazement.

"So just let me get this straight. Brendan will happily watch your sister having sex with one or more other men? And what about him? Does Brendan have relationships with other women?"

Darlene waited for a moment to reply.

"A couple or three years back, they joined a swingers club in Goulburn. I think they are still members. It changed both their lives.

"Bella gets quite turned on watching Brendan fuck other women just as he likes watching her with other men. I should also mention here that Brendan is very well endowed, his cock being bigger and more beautiful than most. Not only that, he is a good and sensitive lover and enjoys pleasuring women. The upshot has been that Brendan will sometimes get a call from a woman that they both know from the swingers club who will say that she is feeling lonely and could they meet up? And most often they do, usually at the farm and with Bella's approval.

"Bella will sometimes join them, usually over in the old disused

Creamery, a nearby building which has been turned into an unofficial bonking venue, complete with mattresses and cushions. Knowing each other means that Bella has probably been with that woman's husband at the monthly swingers get together.

Jessica was fascinated with what Darlene was telling her. Could this possibly be true? Jessica tried to understand it all but found it difficult. Meanwhile, a tiny separate voice at the back of her mind kept wondering how Darlene knew so much about Brendan's penis.

"And then there is Gary, Brendan's younger brother. He manages Muta West but spends quite a bit of time with the rest of them at Muta East. Along with Brendan, he is a trained pilot so he fly's the company plane between the two properties carrying freight and staff to Cobar when needed.

"Gary has a girlfriend here at Muta East, Gina, who is also Bella's best friend. She manages the kitchen and domestic staff. Gary and Gina follow much the same rules as his brother and Bella and so the two are quite happy to watch each other having sex with someone else. I sometimes think that Gina is even more active than Bella, if that were possible.

"There darling. I think I've covered most of the more blatant behavioural oddities of the people you are going to spend a bit of time with. Just don't be too shocked if you see odd things happening with other folk, too."

Jessica commented how Darlene's story had been truly amazing and that now she didn't know whether to be frightened or excited. Then Jessica asked about the women who worked at Muta.

"Probably around a quarter to a third of the staff are women. All sorts; from girly girls to downright scary looking ones. But as to their sexual preferences, one could never be sure. A sweet girly girl university student and from the landed gentry could be a hardcore lesbian who wants to take you to her room and show you her perfect body, while the one with pink, green and blue cropped hair and heavy metal tattoos could be heterosexual and intent on finding the man of her dreams amongst the shearers and settle down and raise a family. There are all sorts.

Jessica commented quietly that that all sounded most interesting.

"By the way, Darlene, how does Prue fit into all of this. Is she settled and happy?"

"Yes, I meant to tell you. She is in a relationship with a much older woman named Ida, a very similar situation to you and Edith, I guess. I've met Ida and we got on really well. They are both free spirits and have given permission to each other to enjoy other people should the occasion arise. It seems to be working.

Then Jessica asked about the sorts of men she might meet.

"And I take it that there is an interesting cross section of males working there, Darlene, or haven't you noticed?"

Darlene let out a sigh then she giggled.

"You will find whatever takes your fancy, Jess, and it won't take long. You will only have to stroll around the property once with your long legs and you will immediately have your hands full, literally.

"I'm very much hoping to reconnect with two brothers, older men who took me to their cabin when I was there the year before last. They are itinerant shearers and spend two months working at the farm. I just missed them last year. Because of the unseasonably wet weather, they left early to work in another State."

Jessica felt a flush of excitement.

"Tell me why they were memorable, Darlene? They obviously floated your boat."

Darlene giggled again, self-consciously.

"They were probably in their late fifties or early sixties and both gentle giants; around six foot three I'd say. They laughingly told me that they hadn't seen such a good quality beast with an arse like mine since they last sheared on a property in Queensland. Not to be outdone, I answered that I hoped they'd done the right thing by the creature, to which they replied, that they would happily show me what they had done, just to get my expert opinion.

"By then I was charmed by their looks and their physique and good humour and I happily offered to judge their style. They took me home to their cabin and proceeded to fuck me silly right through the night. Their stamina was extraordinary and there being two of them, meant that as one came in me and finished, the other would take his brothers place and keep giving it to me like I was the last whore on earth. But not only that, both men recovered quickly so that with only a short rest between bouts, they would be on me again. And so it went, right through the night. It was then that I understood the meaning of a certain naughty term; cum bucket. I surely was one by next morning.

"They were also very gentle and caring as well as being strong and demonstrative. I can tell you, Jess that a girl couldn't have wanted for more."

Jessica rubbed her crotch and felt the knickers beneath her denim jeans getting wet.

"Oh, Darlene. That sounded so wonderful. That story has made me horny. What were there names, I'll try and find them before you do."

"It sounds crazy Jessica, but I never did get their names, and that could make tracking them down a little difficult but hopefully, not impossible.

When they reached Goulburn, Darlene parked in front of a chemist in the main street, and when she returned minutes later she passed one of two bags to Jessica.

"There, darling! A present! I don't want you to miss out on anything at the farm. I have a strong premonition that your cock fantasies are going come all at once, if you will pardon the pun. In the bag is the active girls essentials collection. Just three items; condoms, lube and wet wipes, oh yes, and little bags for rubbish, if you know what I mean. I think you will enjoy them far more than chocolates."

Jessica screamed her delight and put her arms around Darlene and kissed her.

"Thank you so much, Darlene," then with a mischievous smile, she said, "Every time I use anything in this bag I will think of you, you darling woman."

Darlene drove the car out of the parking bay and continued the journey westward.

"Not long to go now, Jess. We'll be there in around half an hour. And I so hope you are ready to settle in to cock heaven, darling. I'm thinking when you head out for a walk the boys there just won't know what hit them. Come to think of it, nor will the girls."

FARM LIFE SURPRISES

JESSICA COULDN'T HELP THINKING that she was on one of those amazing film sets where everything was enormous and the activities most varied. Not that there was a lot of activity at the moment of their arrival. It was just that getting there after traversing the wide flat empty plains seemed surreal. It was like a town in the middle of a desert. What appeared to be accomodation in the form of cabins, spread along the road in either direction, and there were two large buildings at the end of the cabins. Jessica caught a glimpse between the cabins of another row of cabins at the back.

"Girls to the left and boys to the right is how it generally works. And there are married quarters hidden away at the back. Two cabins on each side of the homestead are reserved for the owners' visitors. The two larger buildings at each end are staff dining rooms. Only one is used except when there are events like open days or sales or when they open up during the tourism season."

The main homestead was at the point of where buildings ran in either direction at an angle. Opposite the homestead was a woodland and a small lake with a boat shed and two small shelter sheds where swimmers and picnickers could escape from the sun or heavy rain.

There was also a lovely old brick building beneath a giant Peppercorn tree and which Jessica thought could be the Creamery.

Visitors and workers didn't just park their vehicles outside the main buildings. Except for people who were quartered in the house or cabins, the workers were all required to park in the large carpark when they arrived at the end of the two kilometre drive-in from the main highway. There were at least twenty cars there and room for twice as many more.

A second and larger empty car park could be seen further over and Darlene explained that this was mainly used for visitors attending the twice yearly stud stock sales as was the aircraft landing strip further out.

A young man and a young woman were unloading supplies from a van but other than that, the street was nearly deserted. Darlene explained that there was shearing being done at the shearing sheds a couple of kilometres away and more than half of the residents would be there. She said another group of men would be working on harvesting equipment in the huge hanger out near the air strip and most of the other residents would be working in the big kitchen next to the first of the workers dining room.

As they drew close to the house, three girls on horses wandered past heading in the other direction. Jessica was excited to see young women riding and commented that she wondered if they learnt when they arrive here or did they already know how to ride.

"Many of the young women are the daughters of farmers and are already experienced with horses. Some attend university then take a year off to do this. Others are usually less educated country girls looking for a better life away from their small communities. In short, being somewhere where their mums and dads can't watch over them."

Jessica was most amused and, thinking of her own situation, commented that she thought that made perfect sense.

Jessica was watching the three riders in the rear vision mirror. She was attracted to the tall thin one with the long pony tail who had returned Jessica's stare when they passed each other. The riders had stopped a little way back and the tall girl sat on her horse and stared back at the car, obviously waiting to see who got out.

Darlene didn't miss Jessica's noticing the lanky ponytailed pretty girl.

"I think you are going to have a good time, Jessica. Most of the girls here swing both ways so be ready for anything."

Darlene parked outside the homestead alongside half a dozen vehicles, a late model luxury people mover, and an older Mercedes Benz, a smaller runabout and three utilities, one quite old and the other two very new.

The front door opened as they approached and three women and two men came out to greet them.

"Jessica," called a familiar voice from long ago.

"Prue! It's been such a long time. Feels like a lifetime. So good to see you.

The two friends from school embraced and then stood back to look at each other.

"You're filling out at last", laughed Prue, looking at Jessica's bosom. "I guess we've both moved on as well. Maybe we've grown up at long last."

Darlene called out a happy hello to her daughter and embraced her, then she introduced Jessica to her sister and brother-in-law and to his brother and his partner. Both the men and the women looked at Jessica closely then at each other and smiled and nodded.

"Well, will we offer her job at Muta and try to talk her into staying", asked Annabelle, smiling knowingly at the other three.

"Not sure yet, darling. We'd best check what she can do first before any decision is made. She might be too straight or maybe too much of a handful. Wouldn't want to cause any disruption around the place."

They all laughed and Jessica grinned and went very red.

Darlene came to her aid, "Don't mind them Jessica, they are just trying to frighten you. Mind you, best keep your wits about you. Unexpected things can have a habit of happening here.

Jessica and Darlene were each given a cabin next door to the main house. The little homes were cute and functional and had a double bed and single bunks in an adjacent room. A kitchen and a bathroom made up the rest. It was all wonderful. Then Jessica thoughts turned to the girl she'd seen on horse. So much going on!

11

BARBECUE SIZZLE

Prue knocked on the door just as Jessica finished hanging her clothes in the wardrobe and when she came in, the two women embraced and unlike all those years back, it was Jessica who pushed Prue up against the wall and put her hand inside the girls pants. The two kissed and then Prue pulled away gently and told Jessica that they must save themselves for later. And when Jessica asked why, Prue told her that it was for two reasons.

Prue told Jessica that tonight was the staff monthly barbecue when everybody got out and had a good time. Then Jessica asked Prue what the second reason was.

"My good friend Mandy texted me and asked if she could meet the new hot chick that arrived this afternoon. Mandy doesn't miss much. She and two friends were riding up the street when mum and you arrived. Mandy said she got the hots for you straight away."

Jessica coloured up and looked abashed.

"Well, if she was the tall skinny one with the pony tail, I'm up for it."

Prue laughed and slipped a hand into Jessica's little bra.

"Randy Mandy is quite a gal. She loves gals and guys and she puts herself out there. She's also got a little slave, Cindy who follows her around and does her bidding, getting Mandy anything she asks for, even blokes. Actually, given half a chance, Cindy is a little performer, too.

"So tonight I'll call for you at around seven-thirty and we'll start by strutting our stuff at the barbecue and hook you up with Randy Mandy. You will love her, I'm sure. I'm meeting up with Ida a little later so forgive me if I just dump you with Mandy and Cindy.

"We will no doubt see the others but mum is on a mission to find two shearers she enjoyed the year before last, so she could well disappear. I hope she finds them.

"Oh yes. Did mum talk to you about aunt Bella? I hope she did. Don't be shocked if you suddenly see Bella behind a tree dressed up in her finery with something in her mouth and something else in her hand. They won't be barbecued chops either, although they will doubtless be meaty and juicy.

"You are in for a good time, Jessica. Now, I've given you my number. Call or text if you are having any problems or need advice. Any questions?"

Jessica was excited by what Prue was telling her and her thoughts were going wild trying to work out the evening ahead.

"Just one question, Prue. What are Brendan, Gary and Gina likely to be doing. Do they get to strut their stuff tonight?"

"Good question. Brendan is very popular with some of the girls here and it's likely that a few couples from their swinging group will turn up. The old Creamery just up on the other side of the road will be unlocked and there are mattresses and cushions on the floor there. Bella will often rendezvous with some of the older shearers there, later in the night. Those men like a bit of comfort.

"Gary and Gina some times swap partners with a couple of the married women that Gina works with in the kitchen and sometimes Gina will hook up with one or a pair of the contracting itinerants and go and have them in their cabins. Gina is as active as Bella and on rare occasions the two will compete for a cock that they both want to try but then they will simply end up sharing it.

"Gary has a penchant for older women and some of the young women here who are from local families, will sometimes introduce him to their mothers or aunts. Like his brother Brendan, he's well liked and seems to be well catered for."

Jessica thanked Prue and they kissed and agreed to see each other later.

Jessica welcomed having time to herself for the first time and discovered that there was a proper bath in the bathroom with a continuous supply of hot water, fed by the nearby Wollondilly river. She bathed in a deep bath, soaking herself in nice smelly bath salts, closing her eyes and dreaming of sucking real men's cocks for the first time, instead of the nice young men back home. Jessica fantasised and got very excited and played with herself with a bar of soap, "Oh, this is all so wonderful," Jessica whispered as she shuddered.

———

Prue knocked on the cabin door and collected Jessica and the two wandered across to the barbecue area under the trees on the other side of the roadway. It was late afternoon and sunny but there was already quite a crowd, most of them older shearers and mechanics and contractors, hungry and looking for a feed. Prue said that the younger ones usually appeared a little later when they could more easily be silly or sexy under the cover of darkness.

A voice called out and suddenly the tall skinny Mandy was standing in front of Jessica with her little side-kick, Cindy just two steps behind her. Prue proceeded to introduce them.

"Jessica, this is Mandy and this is her friend Cindy. Mandy and Cindy, meet Jessica. I'm off to town to collect Ida. We'll be back later so we might see you all then."

Jessica and Mandy stood staring at each other defiantly. Both were around the same height and build and both immediately looked forward to physically dominating the other.

Cindy watched excitedly, knowing that this could end either in a hair pulling fight or a screaming explosion of sexual energy. She would be excited either way, knowing that after her idol had a fight with another girl, she would fuck Cindy long and hard with a dildo. And if the encounter with the other woman ended in a sexual encounter, she would benefit just by laying naked alongside the two of them and letting them play with her, if and when they felt like it.

"Lets go for a walk down to the lake."

Mandy turned away and headed off through the trees with Cindy trailing after her but then Cindy turned, beckoning to Jessica to follow.

They had barely left the barbecue area and were passing through the bushy area that surrounded the lake when Mandy turned and grabbed Jessica by the arm and pushed her up against the smooth trunk of a large gum tree. She kissed Jessica forcibly and pushed a hand roughly up the leg of Jessica's tiny shorts. Then she gasped in surprise as Jessica threw her arms around her and swung Mandy against the tree and put her hand up the girls short skirt, fingering her madly as Mandy sagged and surrendered herself, shocked and excited.

"You fucking mad skinny slut. Come with me."

Mandy took Jessica by the hand and they all but ran to the little swimming shack beside the lake. Inside, mattresses lay on the wood floor and big candles sat on saucers on wooden boxes and Jessica saw that it was another place where lovers came.

In seconds, Jessica was on her back with Randy Mandy on top of her.

"Pull her fucking shorts off, Cindy."

Cindy moved in and deftly unbuttoned and removed Jessica's shorts and her panties.

"Now bitch. Give it to me."

Mandy ground her lower body hard against Jessica and probably because the two were already in a heightened state of excitement, both women came, screaming expletives along with many repeated mentions of the word "yes".

Cindy lay close by. She had pulled off her jeans and knickers and was rubbing herself as she watched. Then she gasped and orgasmed and then she leant over to lightly touch the two lovers.

Jessica and Mandy lay in each others arms, staring into each others eyes. They were in love. They kissed gently and slipped their tongues into each others mouths. Peace prevailed.

Suddenly, Mandy jumped up and reached for her phone.

"Whose for some cock? I'll order a take away."

Jessica watched, amazed as her new lady love texted while laughingly saying to the two women laying prone on the mattresses that it was a good time of day to get cock, and that the males were just heading out on the prowl.

A few minutes later, Mandy's phone beeped and she looked and laughed and passed the phone to Jessica.

"It's on the way darling. Us sluts never had it so good. Do you like it?"

Jessica stared at the picture of a large erection and underneath, the words 'On my way. Three more in ten minutes'. Jessica turned and stared at Mandy and smiled.

"Can I lick your phone, you beautiful bitch?"

Three excited women laughed and groped each other.

"You will have the real thing in your sexy mouth in just a few minutes, my love. Then, when the others arrive, you can suck yourself silly. And Cindy and I will too, won't we Cindy?"

"Ooh yes," replied Cindy in an excited voice.

A shadow filled the entrance and a young man in his mid twenties came in beaming a wonderful friendly smile.

"Here I am and I'm here to help."

"Jessica, this is Paul and Paul this is Jessica. She's visiting for the week."

The two smiled and nodded to each other.

"Who else is coming, Paul? I hope we got in early enough given how many horny women seem to have arrived in Muta for the barbecue."

"George is coming and he's bringing a new guy, a visitor who I haven't met yet. His name is Giovani and his from Sydney. Oh yes! Harry is coming and he might be with his shearer mate, Alec. So is five enough?"

Paul laughed and looked appreciatively at Jessica.

"Well, I guess that will get us girls started. Does it sound okay to you two?"

Jessica and Cindy both laughed and said they agreed that it was a start.

Then suddenly the doorway darkened and there were people everywhere. Jessica remembers Paul taking her hand and putting it on his newly exposed erection and moments later she had her biggest cock ever and her first real cock, well housed in her hungry mouth and kicking off an evening of cock sucking bliss.

The last spoken words Jessica remembered was Mandy calling out that Cindy was in charge of the box of condoms and would happily put the condoms on cocks for those who were too dumb to do it themselves.

Jessica felt Pauls hand gently fingering her pussy, and she blissfully cupped and fondled his balls with both hands and sucked on regardless.

Jessica made a point of occasionally looking across at Mandy and Cindy.

Things were happening very quickly, particularly as far as Cindy was concerned. She was on her knees with a cock in her mouth and a man behind her had his member somewhere between her legs.

Mandy had a cock in her mouth and another in her hand. Her long legs where spread wide apart and swaying in the air and hands were groping her breasts and her pussy. There was a lot of frivolity amongst the men but the girls, for obvious reasons, made few sounds other than sucking noises.

Suddenly, Jessica was shaken from her revelry when Paul gently removed his cock and moved away. For a moment Jessica was confused but then suddenly she looked up at the smiling face of a beautiful swarthy man who was offering her his very large member.

"My name is Giovani. What is yours?"

"I'm Jessica. Pleased to meet you."

The ridiculous formality of their introduction went unnoticed as Giovani offered Jessica his erection and which she accepted with unabashed enthusiasm.

A sudden scream signalled Cindy's orgasm and this is probably what reminded the males that there was more on offer than just being sucked and they took turns getting a condom fitted by the dazed Cindy, who nevertheless, still managed to swallow each cock for a few moments before she deftly fitted a rubber sheath.

Giovani interrupted the daydreaming Jessica and with a purring sexy accent asked her if he might fuck her.

"Oh please do, Giovani," she replied sleepily, happy for the lovely man to do anything he pleased.

Giovani went over to Cindy and smiled his beautiful smile and before he could say hello is cock was first licked then swallowed by the excited young woman and only when he took her head in his hand and removed his cock from her mouth did she cover his manhood with a condom.

Then Giovani returned to Jessica and lifted her legs and lent between them and kissed her and told her how beautiful she was and Jessica sighed and mumbled coyly how beautiful he was. Then he put his fingers to her pussy and opened it gently and rested the head of his cock against it.

Jessica shuddered and she felt her wetness looking for him. Then he arrived slowly, moving the bulbous end of his cock backwards and forwards at her entrance. Jessica gasped and reached up and pulled his head down to kiss him and Giovani pushed his tongue into her mouth and moved it gently around. Then he pushed into her and Jessica felt the full force of his giant penis reaching up to touch her womb and moments later and being already in a heightened stated of excitement, she had the first of the evenings many orgasms.

Jessica would not let Giovani leave her. Not that he wanted to, but when he looked deep into her eyes and asked if she had had enough of him and would she like someone else to visit her, she pulled him tightly to her and told him that he must stay inside her all night and that he was not allowed to leave.

Giovani smiled down at her and said he would like to stay right where he was forever, and the sound of his voice and what he said and what was inside her cunt caused Jessica to cum a half dozen times over the next five minutes, each time, shrieking and pulling him down onto her.

When Giovani eventually came, and he filled his condom, the two entwined bodies parted and they looked around. The place was deserted. Everyone had left. Slowly, he lifted Jessica up and asked her if she would like to join him at the barbecue for something to eat. Jessica said that she would and quickly found her clothes and got dressed.

As they ate their steak and onions from paper plates and drank their cokes and coffee, the two kissed and touched each other. And when it was getting on for midnight and Giovani said that he thought he should let her get on with her evening, Jessica looked at him and pointed to the front door of her cabin on the other side of the road and asked him if he would like to spend the night with her. Giovani happily accepted the offer.

The two showered and laughed and got to know each other as best they could in the short time they had together. Giovani said that he had to leave in the morning but how he wished he could stay longer.

Then they snuggled into the big bed and cuddled up. Jessica immediately felt Giovani's huge erection looking for her beneath the bed clothes and rejoiced. And after she had put a condom on him, Giovani fucked her over the next hour or more, resting sometimes to kiss and talk. Then after her many orgasm and his giant explosion, they settled down and slept.

In the early hours, Jessica awoke to find Giovani's cock rubbing against her belly once more and she knew what she wanted next. Jessica moved down in the bed and took him in her mouth and licked and sucked and then using her mouth and her hands she brought him to the boil, letting him almost drown her as he shot his huge load down her willing throat. Jessica had to remind herself that she wasn't dreaming. Happiness was very real today.

12

COUNTRY DOGGING

It was at a midday lunch in the main house the day after the barbecue. Darlene was there looking sleepy but very happy. And Bella was in a good mood, laughing about the night before and how she'd managed very nicely in the bushes, commenting that there was strong competition at times and on one occasion she'd had to share someone with a slightly tipsy jillaroo who kept saying how she wanted to ride Bella in preference to her favourite mare.

"I told her she could saddle me up anytime she felt the urge. I wonder if she'll try to take me up on my offer. Come to think of it, I remember who she was. I might ask her if she'd like a ride."

Everyone laughed and her sister-in law Gina told her she was a lucky bitch.

"By the way, Bella, I was wondering if I could borrow Brendon on Sunday night. You mentioned that you had something else on in town and because Gary is leaving this afternoon to go to Cobar, I would very much like someone to take me dogging. What do you think. I could go on my own but that is not as much fun."

Bella looked across to where Brendan and Gary were standing talking near the doorway. Bella called out to them.

"Brendan and Gary?"

The two men heard her and looked over.

"Gina wants to go dogging tomorrow and was asking if Brendon could take her. She knows I've got something else on. Is that okay with both of you? Gary? Are you okay with that?"

The brothers looked at each other and smiled.

"Fine by me, Bella as long as Gina is happy," Gary answered.

"I'm fine with it but you will have to take the ute, darling. Gina and we will need the van because it looks like there could be a shower or two.

"Okay Gina. It's settled. Just make sure he doesn't get into any trouble and that you bring him back with all of his bits."

Jessica had been watching and listening to this conversation with interest. She turned to Darlene and asked her in a low voice, what on earth were they talking about?

Darlene looked a little confused, not sure how to answer the question. Then she told Jessica about dogging and watched as Jessica's face took on a look of amazement.

Darlene explained that the name didn't come from the doggy, girl-on-her-knees love-making position but from men telling their wives they were taking the dog for a walk, it being an excuse for going to a public space where certain things were going on. As it was currently practiced at dogging events around the country, it was in no way woman friendly. Darlene said she could identify with the theory, that some women might enjoy getting physical attention from more than one man at a time and how they might be turned on by doing things publicly and in front of an audience. But then she went in to say that in many instances that she had heard about, women seem to be coerced by their partners into partaking in a very uncaring and unsatisfying sexual adventure.

"I'm given to understand by Bella, though, that this group is totally different and the people who show up are a more exclusive and selective and caring crowd. They meet under the pine trees at a disused church half way between here and town. It's on private property so that the public doesn't have access. The people are mostly from town, professional people and business folk along with a few wealthy farmers. A few of them are in Bella and Brendon's swinger group. The people are all older, some are widows and widowers, and there are a lot of single men who have never married, usually farmers. And there are a couple of single women who have never been married and who apparently are comfortable interacting with men or women.

"If they were dogging any where else, say at any old public dogging venue, a woman would generally want a man with her as protection, but because this venue is like a gated community with most of the people knowing each other, Bella said quite a lot of women feel comfortable coming on their own if they are single or their husbands are not feeling up to it or are doing something else.

"Some women will come together in the one vehicle apparently, which sounds sensible and possibly even more fun.

"I really must go along one day. It would be interesting to see women honestly enjoying themselves and not there because their husbands pushed them into it. I suppose that in this instance it is really just like the swingers club but with fewer inhibitions."

Jessica looked at Darlene's fat red sexy lips.

"So have you tried it, Darlene?"

"Not here, unfortunately, but a couple of years ago, a man I was friendly with invited me to go dogging with him one night to a park in the eastern suburbs of Sydney. It was quite an eye-opener, I must say, and yes, after the first half an hour or so, I actually began to see how I might enjoy it if it wasn't so grubby. It depends a lot on the people that turn up whether or not you have a good time. I would love to go to this one but I'm leaving in the morning so won't be able to."

Jess continued to stare at Darlene's sexy lips.

"I'm still not understanding how things work, if you know what I mean. How do things get started and where?"

Darlene thought for a moment, eyeing Jessica carefully.

"Well, it began in Briton, probably starting when a couple were making out in their car in a carpark one evening and discovered that they were being watched through the car windows by what seemed like some pervy men, some of whom were exposing and playing with themselves.

"Instead of asking the men to go away, the couple began doing more sexual things together, partly as a joke and then simply to entertain the onlookers. From there it moved on to lowering the window so that men could put a hand in and touch the woman's breasts and from there, it wasn't long before women were enjoying touching the mens cocks. So now dogging sort of follows that historic format. Entertaining an audience outside the car and then, depending on circumstance, allowing them to participate in the action.

"Any questions, darling? Fire away. I'm getting fired up thinking about it.

Jessica laughingly whispered that that was enough to wet everything including her appetite, and that she was already in full dogging mode.

"You might like to ask if you could go along just for the experience. It's a wonderful opportunity to see it happening in a safe environment. And you only have to watch Gina. She is always so enthusiastic about anything she does. Seeing her having fun would be a turn on I'm sure.

"Because you are so much younger than the women who attend you probably won't be expected to participate. Unless you wanted too, of course. You would certainly command an enthusiastic line up at the car window if you did. I guess you could claim to be a university student working on a project on sexuality in older people, or something. "

With those last few words, she looked closely at Jessica with a bemused smile.

The two women laughed and Jessica found herself thinking about it, a bit more than she would have expected.

As the Saturday morning get-together came to an end, Jessica nervously approached Gina who was talking to Brendan. The two looked up at Jessica and smiled. Gina spoke first.

"Hope you had a good night last night Jessica. Heard you hung out with Randy Mandy and Cindy. Great gals. They would have kept you busy, I bet."

Gina glanced down at the lower half of Jessica's body appreciatively, and quietly commented that she hoped she had been appreciated by the local lads.

Jessica coloured up and replied that she had had a great night and had no regrets.

"I just wanted to ask you both if it would be possible for me to come with you tomorrow night. Darlene has been telling me about dogging and now I desperately want to know more. I thought that, if needs be, I could say I was a university student working on a project about sexuality in older Australians, or something. But would it be rude to go along as just an observer? Please be honest. I don't want to cause any trouble or difficulties."

Brendan spoke first.

"Well, I'm okay with it but I think it's really up to Gina. She'll be holding centre stage so she should be the one making the decision. What do you think, Gina?"

Once again Gina gave Jessica the once over, and smiled warmly.

"I think we could take her. She might have to wear a poncho for a while, to hide her charms and not be competition for me. But I can handle that. Yes, come along and extend your education sweetie. And if you want to join in, well I won't get upset. I'll probably just grab you like I will be doing to everyone else."

Everyone laughed and Jessica thanked them.

"We'll be leaving from out the front at eight-a-clock. You will be in the passenger seat as Gina will be in the back seat. Okay with that, Gina? Is there anything else we should tell Jessica?"

"Only that it looks like it will be a warm night but bring a jacket in case it turns chilly. And finally, if you don't think you are up for joining in then best not to dress up too much. Not that it really matters except heels and stockings will quickly get the men going, and if you are not interested in getting involved, you might regret having worn them.

"And if you do find yourself getting excited and you want to join in, we're there for you."

Jessica decided to have an early night and was the first to say her farewells as dinner came to a close.

The crowd at the table had been jovial and raucous and she had very much enjoyed their company.

She and Prue sat together along with Prue's partner Ida, and Jessica couldn't help but notice how the older Ida so reminded her of her own partner, Edith, and she wondered about how Prue's situation had come about, given the unusual circumstances surrounding her and Edith's discovery of each other.

She would inquire about it later when she and Prue were alone together.

Sunday dawned and Jessica showered and went off to the lake for a walk.

A mist rose off the water and cockatoos and galahs screamed from the gum trees. It was truly a beautiful time of day and Jessica wondered what it must be like living here. Then she reminded herself that every place was wonderful but the longer one stayed the more every day seemed like a day anywhere, regardless of the attractions.

She recalled the wonder of her first few months living in Sydney, and whilst she still loved it very much, Jessica rarely awoke with the same excited feeling of expectation she had when she first arrived there.

Then Jessica started to sort things through in her head; the adventure she was going to have this evening, then a brief moment of thinking about the lovely Giovani followed by another sudden vision, this time of Mandy's legs wide apart and waving in the air.

But mostly Jessica's mind focused on what she had learnt about dogging. Scary as it might seem, many men exposing their cocks to her outside the window of a car couldn't help but make her want to touch herself. Then Jessica revisited that glimpse of Gina looking at her and the attractive woman's smile of appreciation as she scanned Jessica's long body. The thought that Gina wanted her, unexpectedly excited her and she thought about the woman and her comely body and that delicious smile radiating above the woman's alluring cleavage.

The saying that you get what you think about repeated itself again when there was a knock on the door in the early afternoon. "Come in," Jessica called out.

Gina came in and, smiling, walked over to her and without saying a word, took Jessica in her arms and kissed her. Jessica responded, putting her arms around the well built, almost maternal figure. Then to Gina's surprise and before the woman could make a move, Jessica slid a hand up inside Gina's blouse that hung loosely over her jeans, discovering to her surprise, that Gina's huge bosom was being held up by a bra that had holes for her nipples to protrude from. And protrude they did, standing out like little thumbs.

"Oh God! You are the horny little creature I'd picked you for," uttered Gina, gasping from the feeling of Jessica's fingers on her nipples.

Jessica lifted the blouse and looked at the amazing bust and the even more amazing brasier.

"Gina! I so love your bra. How magnificent your tits look. That is so exciting."

Gina laughed out loud and pushed Jessica backwards so that she could see her face.

"These are the latest thing for some of our ladies at dogging. Delvene at the lingerie shop in Goulburn got them for us.

"The larger ladies with big tits are all a bit self-conscious when they see themselves hanging down or swinging about when they are on their knees and being energetically exercised from the rear. Delvene looked into it and came up with these. The ladies love them and so do their men. The girls show them off to each other sometimes when they arrive at the venue. And some have said that they wear them at home because the bra is a turn on for their husbands resulting in them getting much more attention.

"Delvene has also said that she had something else on order for us to check out. Butt lifter crotchless pants. Now how exciting is that?"

Jessica put her mouth over a nipple and Gina squirmed.

"Now, Jessica. You've made my visit a lot easier. Thank you. I came to ask if you would ride in the back of the van with me on the way to dogging tonight, instead of in the front with Brendan.

"Normally, when Gary takes me, I sit in the front on the way there and unzip him and play with him. It warm me up and makes me hot to trot as soon as I get there. It makes it so much better if you're wet already. I haven't been able to stop thinking about you since we met, and if you would be so kind as to ride in the back with me until we got there, I'm sure that would properly warm me up so that I'd be well and truly ready for my first cock when we arrived. Then you can just hop into the front passenger seat before anyone came over, and hide under the poncho if you need to. Will you do that, Jessica?"

It was a no brainer and Jessica laughed and said how she would be honoured to have the opportunity to warm Gina up. The two laughed and kissed some more and Gina couldn't resist running her hand up Jessica's legs and groping her small and perfect bum.

"You are so beautiful Jess."

Jessica slipped a hand down over Gina backside, appreciating the size and feel of her large firm buttocks.

"Can I ask you something, Gina?"

"Anything you want Jess. Fire away."

The two women sat on the edge of the bed and held hands.

"Well! I've only recently sucked off a my first couple of cocks and I did enjoy it. I experienced a thrill of a sort which I can't explain to myself. It got me wondering what you feel when you are sucking all those cocks at a dogging event. I'm in two minds about it. On the one hand I'm horrified at the idea and on the other, I'm intrigued and realise that you must be doing it for a reason. Can you help me with this, Gina? Can you tell me what it really is that makes you want to do it? Am I too inexperienced to understand it yet?"

Gina stared into space, obviously trying to think through what Jessica had asked.

"You probably know, Jessica, that what you see of a woman's clitoris is really only a tiny part of a huge web of nerves running all over the place, even up to the anus. Ask any woman who enjoys anal sex.

Scientists say that a woman's genitals are home to more than eight thousand nerve endings.

"There is the belief that women crave many cocks for a variety of reasons, be it an unhappy childhood, bad self-esteem, or in the case of dogging, because they are at heart, exhibitionists who get a thrill from being watched by other people while having sex.

"I can't speak for any of those reasons specifically but there is a common thread running through the swinging and dogging community and that is that men, despite claiming that they don't get enough, are in fact far less sexual than women. Once a man as ejaculated, he's finished, at least for quite a while and not only physically. He losses emotional interest entirely, avoiding any sort of touching or intimacy until the next time he wants sexual release.

"Women are totally different physiologically. They are sensitive to erotic feelings for a much longer period and this can often give them pleasure in many parts of the body simply by touching.

"That pleasure, a sort of sustained mini orgasm can, in my opinion, be even more enjoyed as the result of sucking a man off.

"In my experience, sucking and tossing off a man provides a sort of sexual transference from the man to the woman. When I'm holding and tossing off a cock I will automatically sense when the man is about to cum and knowing this, feelings begin to act on my genitals so that at the moment of his orgasm, I get an intense feeling deep down resulting in a chain reaction of continuous euphoric sensations.

"Does that make sense, darling?"

Jessica stared at Gina with adoring eyes.

"Oh yes, Gina."

Then Jessica pushed Gina back on the bed and climbed on top of her and did her violent shagging movement, taking the two to lovers heaven.

Gina lay back, her eyes ablaze.

"You are definitely warming me up tonight, Jessica, and those poor men will wonder what's got into this ravenous creature with the extraordinary bra."

Brendan wasn't really surprised when, on opening the passenger door for Jessica, Gina called out.

"No Brendan. Pop her in here. Jessica's warming me up tonight."

Over the twenty minute drive to the old church, Gina showed Jessica what she was wearing under her full length coat.

Oh you are truly beautiful, gasped Jessica, looking at Gina in her corselet, suspenders and stocking and high heeled shoes. And then there was the black bra with the large holes displaying not just her nipples but also the large chocolate areola that surrounded them.

Jessica immediately thought of a chocolate ice-cream topped with a large treat of some kind.

The two women kissed and fondled one another and in what seemed only minutes, Brendan announced their arrival.

Gina gave Jessica one last kiss, then she lifted her legs and removed her panties.

"A girl is not dogging until she removes her knickers."

And with much laughter and a final kiss, Jessica got out and moved into the passenger seat in the front. She looked at Brendan and he leant across and pulled a clear plastic poncho over Jessica's head to help hide her and it was just as he did that and Jessica bent her head, she looked down and was shocked to see that he had his cock out of his trousers and it was standing very stiff.

Brendan suddenly realised that he was exposed to someone who was new to dogging.

"Sorry, Jessica. Blokes have to warm up too. I would have been in the back but you were there, so I had to do it on my own."

Brendan moved to put his cock away but before he could manage it, Jessica had reached out and was clasping it tightly.

"Would you mind if I helped you warm up just a little bit more, Brendan?" Jessica whispered.

Then a laugh from the back and Gina commented.

"Well, Jessica. You managed to get hold of one before me. Well done."

Then in a different voice, the lady in the back announced that her first customer had arrived and Jessica just heard the electric window going down.

"Hello, Harry! Have your brought me something. Oh yes, I can see you certainly have. It's looking very appetising too. Come a bit closer love."

Jessica's head was full of swirling images. She now had a hand on Brendan's cock and Gina was about to enjoy Harry, whoever Harry was, through the back window. She needed to make sense of things; to work out what she was going to do with all that was going on.

Brendan looked at Jessica with a loving smile.

"I'll have to leave you shortly, Jessica. Not that I don't want to be with you but I do have an appointment somewhere else which I must attend to."

A voice came from the back seat.

"That'll be with that randy Daphne. Don't think I don't know Bren. She's got a soft spot for you. Have fun."

Then Jessica heard a more muted voice from the backseat, "I think we're nearly there Harry. Are you ready?"

And then only moments later, after Harry had yelled "Yes", Gina with a new voice spoke again.

"Hello Tom. Don't go away love. You're next."

When Brendan left the car, Jessica could hardly wait to look between the seats to the back, at what was going on there. She heard a man groan and saw Gina thrusting his cock down her throat and she saw the man's mask-like face as he came. Within seconds, Gina had reached out to another stiff cock nearby and was drawing it in towards her.

Jessica was excited beyond belief. She'd had a cock in her hand just a moment ago but it had got away. Now she desperately wanted another one. She leaned over the back of the seat. Gina already had a second cock in her other hand which she stroked lovingly.

"Gina? I want to put my window down too. Is that all right with you. Just say if it's not."

Jessica heard a stifled sound then Gina's voice.

"Go for it girl. There is plenty around tonight. I'm going to open the door on the other side shortly anyway. I need to offer my other end. The boys deserve the full menu."

Jessica absorbed what Gina had said and then she thought about what the woman had said earlier.

"A girl is not dogging until she removes her knickers."

Jessica lifted her backside off the seat and slipped her panties off.

And yes, the minute she did that she felt different. Then she removed herself from the poncho. Then she heard Gina's muffled voice again.

"Show your tits darling. That will bring them closer."

Obeying her dogging guru was now the order of the day and Jessica pulled the tiny straps down over her shoulders, and let her cotton dress drop to her belly and leaving her small tight pointy breasts on display to the world.

Then that quiet voice came from behind came again.

"Let the back of your seat down a bit so that you can lean back to show off."

Then the voice was gone leaving just the sounds of Gina sucking and gurgling.

With the back of the seat adjusted, Jessica nestled back and glanced down at her breasts. Then, out of the corner of her eye she noticed something moving. Two stiff cocks were swaying and lifting up and down beside her, against the passenger door window and a little voice inside Jessica screamed with delight.

As Jessica was about to press the button to let down the window, Gina's voice spoke again.

"Don't rush darling. Tease them a bit. You will enjoy it and they'll get even stiffer."

The message made Jessica slow down. She smiled sweetly at the two cocks and the faces above them. Then she pressed the button and let the window down about a third of the way.

A hand and arm came through and began to caress Jessica's breasts and she closed her eyes to savour the moment when she made her first dogging contact. Then a second hand came in and tried to reach down to lift the hem of her dress but couldn't quite reach.

Jessica opened her eyes and looked at the arms and hands reaching out for her.

Gina had said to tease them and Jessica was excited about that. She slowly put a hand down and lifted the hem of her frock up over her belly. Her small matt of auburn hair covering her pussy was now on display and she sensed the excitement outside the window. Jessica glanced through the window and was shocked to see five or more cocks attempting to get her attention. This was a lot more than she had envisaged and she wasn't sure what to do.

"Hold and suck one while you hold and rub another. Don't try to do too much. Just finish off one at a time."

Jessica realised that she was in love with Gina. How could she not be. With a slight feeling of trepidation, Jessica lowered the window so that she could reach the men. In just moments, there was a hand on her pussy and she found herself pushing against a man's inserted fingers and with her legs wide open.

Then she made a move. Jessica reached out and took the closest cock into her hand and began to rub it. Then she took another one with her other hand and suddenly she was rubbing two big stiff cocks and admiring each one for its colour and shape. The first stuck straight out while the second had a definite bend upwards. And the purple veins that ran around each were pulsating and calling to her.

Jessica became aware that Gina had opened the other side door, and taking time out for a cursory look behind showed her that Gina was on her knees and a gentleman was kneeling behind her waving his cock. Jessica couldn't help but hear the conversations, especially the low reassuring voice of Gina.

"Just pop it in Henry. You know how I love to have you in my pussy. And go as hard as want lover boy. I'm hungry for it. And the condoms are where they always are, in that box on the floor."

And then to someone in front of her, "Hello Bernie. Got something for me I hope? How is Mildred? Is she back home yet. Dreadful business. Now we just need to get you relaxed and wanting to give me that little present you know I love. Lets just tickle you under here. Would you like that?"

Jessica found herself smiling and appreciating this amazing woman's easy going but supper sexy manner. She wondered if she could ever be like Gina.

Jessica was brought back to her situation when she suddenly realised that the cock in her mouth was about to cum. And then she felt it. That tingling feeling in her pussy and elsewhere as the man pushed in to her mouth and shot his semen down Jessica's throat. Then he was gone and the cock in her other hand was pushing itself towards her mouth and feeling quite ready to cum and suddenly and just in time, Jessica took another load of cum into her, tingling all the way down and around her genitals.

And the cocks kept coming. By the time Brendan returned and Gina had said her goodnights and closed her doors, Jessica figured that she had sucked at least a dozen cocks and felt a similar number of different hands on her tits and between her legs.

Gina pushed her head between the seats and kissed Jessica on the cheek.

"Well done, darling. I got the feeling that you might have enjoyed it. Am I right?"

Jessica lifted a hand to Gina's face and caressed her cheek.

"Yes I did, Gina. And I even felt what you had described earlier. Thank you."

Brendan arrived and got into the drivers seat.

"Everyone okay? Ready to head home?"

Gina reached a hand through and felt Brendan's trouser front.

"Yes, yes! It's still there, Gina. By the time we get home and you've had a shower I'll be ready to finish you off. I promise."

Gina smiled in the darkness then spoke.

"I can't really speak for Jessica but she has been busy while you were away having yourself some fun. She might like to be finished off, too.

"It happens a lot, Jessica. Bella and I, like most women, enjoy being properly shagged when we get home. Our finishing off as we call it. Do you have thoughts about having something like that, darling. An optional extra, I call it."

Jessica smiled and remembered Brendan's lovely cock that she had in her hand only momentarily earlier in the evening.

"If there is enough to go round, I'd love to be finished off."

Brendan and Gina laughed heartily.

"Make that two finishing offs, please driver."

"Certainly, Madam. My pleasure."

A MAN OF THE CLOTH

IT WAS a late Friday afternoon as Brendan delivered Jessica to the bus station at Goulburn. She had said her teary goodbyes to everyone and promised to come back again soon. Even Mandy had shed a tear, calling her a bloody slut who should live here with people who understood her.

Prue said she would be in Sydney in a few weeks to stay with her mum and that it would be nice to catch up then. And Gina winked and whispered that she would miss her and made her promise that she would go dogging with them again and do her the favour of warming her up beforehand. Jessica, hugged her and told her she would and thanked her for showing her the way forward.

"I will never forget what you've taught me, Gina. Thank you."

Whether it was that last moment with Gina or something else, Jessica put on her 'finery' as Bella called it, her stockings and high heels and her very short skirt and happily jumped into the utility when Brendan tooted from outside her cabin.

"Wow! Is there something going on that I haven't been told about? Brendan said, looking at Jessica appreciatively.

Jessica leant across and kissed him on the cheek.

"If there was, Brendan, I'd make sure that you were the first to know."

The quick ride into the bus station was very pleasant. Brendan talked about the farm and how managing during the drought had been extremely difficult. And when Jessica enquired about the swingers club, Brendan talked about how he and Annabella had decided to join the club some three years back and how that had impacted on their lives. He said how it had brought them closer together and how that now they watched out for each others emotional needs much more than they had before.

"It's so enriched our lives," he said. He went on to tell how both he and Annabella shared thoughts about other people and potential lovers. Each wanted to see the other enhance their lives and that making love to other people did just that.

At the bus terminal, the big coach was already sitting with its motor ticking over and most of the passengers had already found seats. Jessica farewelled Brendan in the half light of early evening and as they hugged, she said how she had enjoyed her visit far beyond her expectations.

Jessica climbed aboard the luxury coach and presented her ticket to the driver. Then she wandered along the aisle until she found a seat towards the back. The window seat was occupied by what appeared to be a priest or vicar in black clothing and with a white dog collar. He looked up and smiled and Jessica thought how handsome he was and put the man's age in the early to mid thirties.

Jessica deliberately turned her back towards the man and bent over pretending to look for something in her bag before sitting down, hoping that he had taken the opportunity to look at her long legs and appreciate her tight short skirt.

As Jessica settled in to the soft padded seat and started to roll the images of the past week through her mind she was suddenly amused when it occurred to her that if she had been a catholic and the man next to her was a priest, he might have enjoyed listening to her confession.

With an almost silent purr, the coach moved off, the bus interior lights were dimmed for the evening and Jessica watched the last moments of the setting sun across the vast empty plains.

After about twenty minutes, when Jessica was sitting with her eyes closed and playing out a scene in her mind of Mandy with her legs in the air, she felt a gentle touch on her knee. The initial shock was immediately followed by her sharp sucking in of breath, the sound of which Jessica managed to stifle. Then she allowed herself the thrill of accepting that the priest was interested in getting to know her better, and remembering that it was only recently she had come to understand the excited feeling she got in her head and her groin when men wanted her, when they longed to touch her. Jessica was soon on fire.

Then Jessica remembered the wise words of her teacher, Gina, when they were in the car dogging and Jessica was staring through the car door window at her first line-up of cocks. "Don't rush darling. Tease them a bit. You will enjoy it and they will get even stiffer."

Jessica looked down in the dim light of the bus and could just make out the priests fingers lightly touching her leg and moving slowly up towards the hem of her skirt, and she smiled inside, knowing she had a man all to herself for the next couple of hours.

Jessica sat back and savoured the moment. The man's fingers softly rubbing her stockinged legs felt so beautiful. Then Jessica thought about the situation and realised that, while the journey was going to take another couple of hours, she couldn't be sure how far her admirer would go. She decided that she had time to wait a little while before responding and noted how his fingers were already up under her skirt, softly rubbing and pushing down between her inner thighs.

Jessica wondered what he would think when her groper discovered that she wasn't wearing knickers, and she smiled at the thought; that was if he could get past just wanting to play with her suspenders. Men totally love suspenders according to her sex guru, Gina.

Two fingers reached her crotch, and met a little bush of hair and stopped. Then they moved down to discover Jessica's already very wet vagina and two fingers slipped inside her.

It was time for Jessica to make a move. It must be obvious to the man that Jessica was happy with what he was doing, she reasoned. Now it was her turn.

Jessica half turned and moved an arm across and placed her hand on the priests trousers, finding a sturdy lump which moved violently when she touched the spot where it was buried.

Not to be backward in coming forward, Jessica moved her second hand down to where the man was feeling her pussy and she pressed him in further, signalling her approval of his wanton but much appreciated action.

A hand removed Jessica's hand from her spot on the trousers and she sensed a flurry of activity in the semi-darkness as the priest extricated his member. Then he reached over and took Jessica's hand and placed it on his liberated cock and Jessica rejoiced, knowing that her quiet time on the bus was going to be well spent.

Jessica pulled her hand upward and gently massaged the head of the priests cock with her finger tips. She was in no hurry. Jessica listened as the thousands of nerve endings in her genitals celebrated the actions and she shivered with the intense excitement she felt at the proposition of sucking the priest off.

Her man of the cloth, having received confirmation of Jessica's approval of his actions was now enlivened and he rubbed her pussy enthusiastically. Jessica responded and rewarded him by slightly lifting her abdomen and thrusting it forward onto his fingers. She even put her hand down onto his and took another finger and put it in herself to join the other two. Three fingers is the best number, Darlene had once told her.

Jessica felt the cock in her hand throb and it suddenly felt bigger and stiffer and she felt saliva trickling into her mouth in preparation for her feast.

When Jessica at last got up on the seat on her knees and put her head down and took the priest into her mouth, the man sighed and stroked the back of her head.

Jessica was impressed with her new acquisition. The cock was not long but it was impressive in its thickness. She lovingly worked her tongue around it, lifting her mouth off of it before plunging it back into her mouth and swallowing it again.

Jessica thought how heavenly this cock felt then found herself smiling at the idea of the priest taking her to heaven. She slid her hand down and rubbed the man's testicles and she heard his soft groan.

While Jessica pushed her lips and mouth all over his cock, the priest was now able to reach over the kneeling woman and pull up her skirt and run his hand over her bottom. He touched her anus and rubbed a finger up and down that little valley that joined her anus and Jessica's vagina and for just a moment, Jessica thought how good it would be if the priest could fuck her. But that wasn't possible and in any case, she was having such a good time with what was already available to her.

Jessica had been sucking and rubbing the priest for almost an hour. His fingers in her cunt had afforded her a few mini orgasms and now, she reasoned, it was probably time to relieve the man of his load. She removed her mouth and began to rub him more vigorously and the priest sensed where she was going and pushed his cock upward in anticipation.

Then came the time when Jessica knew that the man was about to cum and the host of nerve endings excitedly urged her on. Jessica told herself that she should be ready in about thirty seconds and sure enough, the priest gave up his holy message with great force while he clutched Jessica's head so that she could not get away.

Jessica had no desire to escape and lovingly slurped the exhausted member, licking everything and sucking gently while feeling the heavenly cock slowly subside.

Jessica lifted her head and smiled at the man through the darkness and murmured, "Thank you. I really enjoyed that."

That the priest appreciated Jessica's comment was made clear when he leant forward and kissed her on the lips.

"Thank you, you beautiful girl. I will remember this moment."

When the coach arrived in the Sydney depot, the lights went on and everyone rose to leave. Jessica and the priest looked at each other and Jessica felt herself blushing. Jessica made an effort to speak.

"Are you visiting Sydney or do you live here?" she asked, not really knowing what to say.

The handsome priest swung his small suitcase from the rack above and smiled.

"I'm just here for a visit. I'm going to a fancy dress party tonight. The theme is Changing Ones Occupation. What do you think? Do I look convincing?"

14

THE DUNKING

JESSICA WAS SURPRISED one day when her phone rang and she saw who it was.

"Gina! How lovely to hear from you. What brings you to my phone you adorable lady."

Gina giggled and explained that she was in Sydney and staying with their mutual friend, Darlene. Jessica heard a distant voice calling hello to the telephone and she called back, hello Darlene.

I'm here for a function later in the week to which I thought you might like attend with both of us. If you were free tomorrow, we could both call around and tell you all about it.

Jessica asked if they would like to have a pizza when they arrived and Darlene said they would and with a bit of toing-and-froing with Darlene, gave Jessica their preferred pizza toppings order.

"We'll see you at about five thirty, darling. Bye!"

The two larger than life women arrived at Jessica's small flat and made themselves comfortable.

"Oh I do wish I was young and fancy free again, don't you, Darlene?"

Darlene and Jessica laughed and Jessica said it had its advantages but she doubted they made up for the exciting lives that the two women seemed to enjoy.

"She's even got a couple of lads on tap in the flat across the hallway who will appear at her bidding," Darlene whispered loudly, suggesting this was a well kept secret.

Gina looked at Jessica with a glowing smile.

"I will have to visit more often, I can see that."

Jessica coloured up and deflected further comment by asking what event she was being invited too, later in the week.

"Well, darling. Sit back and I'll explain. And I will understand if you choose not to come."

Gina then launched into her story about a woman named Sally who she had known for many years but now only saw occasionally when she visited Goulburn with her husband, Claude. She told how Sally had a brother who farmed near Goulburn and that he and his wife were friends of Annabella and Brendan. These friends were also a part of Bella and Brendan's swinger group and were regular attendee's at the dogging events under the pine trees at the disused church.

Sally's husband, Claude, was a property developer in Sydney.

"A year ago, the husband acquired a very large open-span warehouse that had previously been used as one of those giant budget furniture outlets.

"Claude wasn't quite sure what he was going to do with the property, but it was available at such a low price, he simply bought it, thinking he would work out a use for it later, or simply sell it on at a profit when prices for industrial properties rose.

"Eventually Claude had the sudden idea that he would turn it into an indoor camping site. Inspired, he rushed to put in a pool and a sauna and a playground and he was even planning to get some pet wallabies and have aviary bred cockatoos flying around inside the cavernous building.

"It sounded ridiculous at the time but he loved the idea of people being able to camp all the year round and without going very far.

"Claude sealed the whole factory with that soft spongy asphalt stuff we sometimes see on footpaths. He laid out car parking spots, each with a space for a tent and with a small bench and table. All were numbered so that spots could be assigned to a family who joined.

"It was only after his grown-up children took him aside and explained about the real reasons why people went camping, that he changed his ideas.

"He was in the middle of coming up with some other use for the place when he suffered a heart attack and died.

"Sally was eventually face with selling up his properties, but when she visited the warehouse with the accountant and saw how much Claude had done, she knew what to do."

Gina stopped talking to take a deep breath.

"Sally and Claude had, since the very beginning, attended the dogging sessions at our church site near Goulburn and they had loved it.

"Sally suddenly envisaged the warehouse as a gated dogging site and without further ado, threw herself into organising it with the same vigour as Claude had with his camp site plans.

"Everything was going fine, she put in a lighting system that allowed itself to be turned into bright moonlight, and even added clusters of large indoor ferns in huge containers.

"But Sally realised that she had one problem. How to get enough men to make it interesting for the ladies. After all, the whole thing was supposed to be female friendly and she wanted to be certain that their needs would be met.

"The enjoyable experiences she had had at our little dogging sessions at Goulburn where made possible by the fact that we had a large number of widowers and bachelors as members, as well as the women and their husbands.

"Where to get men and more importantly, the right men?"

Gina stopped talking again and rested. Jessica looked at Darlene and smiled and said how exciting Gina's story was and how she so hoped that it would have a happy ending. Darlene laughed and said she thought they would be finding out very soon.

"It was a stroke of luck that Sally was introduced to the owner of

The Club, a newly opened female friendly club where men and women, and women and women, could meet up during the day for sexual encounters. Incidently, I understand that it is located not far from here, Jessica?

"The owner, Desley Leigh had heard about the doggers at Goulburn from the member who introduced her to Sally, and she thought it sounded interesting.

"The upshot of this meeting - and after numerous get togethers between the two women and their accountants - was that Desley would offer her members, both male and female, a voucher giving them two free nights at Sally's new venture which, by the way, she had named The Dunking, a name she chose in an effort to move people away from the original dogging label yet still sound suggestive. She had moments of considering other names, like Donuts & Dunking, but eventually settled for the shorter name after talks with Desley.

"The signed agreement outlined that Sally's business should not compete with The Club so that it should not open before 7 pm in the evenings and never be open during the day.

"This arrangement was agreed to resulting in a trebling of the number of males who turned up at The Dunking's opening and was pivotal to the enormous success which The Dunking now enjoyed."

"Finally, ladies, I have an invitation for myself and two friends to attend The Dunking tomorrow night. So are you both up for it?"

Darlene looked at each of the two women and then back at Jessica.

"I'm definitely up for it. What about you, Jessica?"

"Count me in. I'm already hot just thinking about it."

Gina, Darlene and Jessica all agreed that The Dunking private dogging venue looked truly amazing. As they stared out of the car windows while lining up to have their credentials checked, they slowly edged forward through the double gates and looked down on a sea of cars and tents.

The time was only seven fifteen. A large sign at the entrance advised that a gong would sound at eight o'clock at which time the lights would be turned down to a bright moonlight level at which point, attendees could begin the fun part of the evening. A second sign cautioned against bringing alcohol or drugs to the venue. It also asked that peoples radios and phones remain switched off until the end. Photographs were forbidden.

The sounding of the gong also signalled that from the that moment on, women were required to be dressed or at least covered with a robe if they were wandering around outside the painted lines marking the perimeter of their allocated campsite. Men were also expected to be modest and keep things inside their trousers when wandering between locations.

People roamed about looking at each other and at the vehicles and various features of the venue. Some were standing at the buffet over at the far wall, enjoying snacks. Others were inspecting one of the twelve repainted kombi vans that the owner had bought from a wrecking yard and positioned around the place.

As well as being painted in bright colours, the vans had been stripped of their back seats and then carpeted throughout, including the raised engine cover area at the back. The passenger door and drivers door had newly fitted electric windows, replacing the old rusted up manual windows. The front seats had been recovered and the long upright gearstick removed.

The kombis' were placed within the boundaries of a dozen numbered sites and were available for hire by those who wanted more room.

As Gina drove into the assigned parking space she announced that she had rented the kombi van parked beside them.

Jessica screamed with excitement.

"It has always been a big regret that I was born to late to rumble in a kombi. Now my prayers have been answered. Oh God, I'm warming up already."

The two older women laughed, enjoying Jessica's enthusiasm.

"Well, darling. You might have to share it with two experienced kombi ladies. What do you think, Gina? Will we let her put her lovely body on the floor of the van with us?"

"Of course Darlene, just so long as she shares her suitors with us if we're not getting enough attention."

Much laughing ensued and Jessica called them rude names.

"I'm so young and I have much to catch up on to catch up to you two. It would help me if you left my conquests alone so that I could get a full experience. You wouldn't want me to have less than a proper education, would you?"

Everyone got out of Gina's large people carrier to look around. The place really was like a camping ground.

Smiling women and men passed by, looking closely at the three newcomers.

The crowd seemed so clean and middle class and a woman could be forgiven for thinking that these men could never act in a demonstrative and sexy manner.

Perhaps she would find them boring, thought Jessica.

"Only five minutes to go girls. Are we just about ready?"

Gina went and stepped into the open double doors of the yellow, green, and orange kombi. First she laid down on the carpeted floor. Then she got up and turned and leant over the raised carpeted motor cover at the back of the van. She lifted her skirt and called out.

"How do I look, girls."

The two women stared at Gina's brazen display, appreciating her delightful rear end and Darlene clapped. Then Jessica remembered Gina's advise to her when they were dogging in Goulburn.

"I was once told by an expert that a girl is not dunking until she removes her knickers, Gina."

As Jessica finished speaking, a loud gong sounded and the lights dimmed. And in the new soft light, Gina laughed and slipped her knickers off.

"Everybody to their positions. Time to go and enjoy ourselves girls. Best of luck."

Darlene looked at Jessica.

"I fancy the back seat of the van we came in, Jessica. I need to spread myself. Is that okay with you?"

"Sure thing. I'm going to start where I finished up on my first time; the front seat of the van. Okay with you, Darlene?"

The two took their positions and looked out at the still milling crowd.

"Knickers off then, Jessica?"

"That would be a start, Darlene. Plus the other thing Gina told me."

"What was that, darling?"

"Show your tits darling. That will bring them closer."

Darlene laughed and said what good advice that was. She laid back on the wide back seat and unbuttoned her blouse, displaying her big breasts held in by an enormous lacy bra, and then she lifted the hem of her skirt to display her stocking tops and her red suspenders.

Jessica pulled down the long rear vision mirror that Brendan had installed - his perving mirror he called it - so that she could occasionally check on Darlene. She saw her friend laid out in all her finery.

"Oh Darlene, I think I want to join you, you sexy bitch."

Jessica unbuttoned her top and looked down at her small shapely breasts.

Suddenly both women had other things to think about and Jessica heard Darlene's soft voice from the back of the van.

"Cock alert, darling."

At that moment, Jessica realised that she had not thought as much about sucking cocks over the past twenty-four hours as she would have normally. It was now a topic close to her heart and a day would rarely pass that she didn't slip into a semi daydream state and imagine herself with her mouth around a fully erect penis.

Since her dogging event at Goulburn, Jessica had come to understand a bit more about a man's magic phallus. She now understood how enjoyable it was to hold the covering skin tightly between her lips while they were stretched over her teeth, and moving his skin covering around and rotate it like a sleeve or a glove, independent of the flesh and muscle that it covered.

Just as Jessica felt herself drifting into her dream state, a sound beside her brought her back to the present. There was a light tapping on the window and outside, two big purple cocks were peering at her through the glass, lifting themselves up and down and sometimes wagging from side to side.

Again, Gina's voice echoed in Jessica's head, "Don't rush darling. Tease them a bit. You will enjoy it and they'll get even stiffer."

Jessica looked above the cocks into the eyes of the neatly dressed men they belonged to. Accountants or middle management she mused. She smiled, and rubbed her hands over her breasts and pushed them out provocatively, then she lifted the hem of her skirt and palmed her pussy then lifted herself up off the seat, wriggling her naked abdomen and her small tuft of hair up close to the window.

The cocks lifted and wagged with excitement and Jessica wanted to purr like a cat. And just like a cat, Jessica wanted to play with these cocks and taunt them until they begged for release.

And who were these men, anyway? And were their partners here too? Were their wives semi naked in vehicles here, touching themselves between their legs while at this very moment, looking at cocks through the window and for the same excitement Jessica was looking for?

Jessica dropped the window so that she could reach out and take a cock in her hand. Two hands dived into the car, one went to her breast and the other between her legs.

As her hand closed around a warm welcoming penis, Jessica felt that magic feeling as the thousands of nerve endings she'd learnt lived in that area around her genitals. Her body quivered and celebrated.

And while gently directing the first willing penis towards her mouth, Jessica chanced a look into the kombi next door.

Gina was kneeling in front of two men. She had a cock in each hand while at her rear end two other men were taking it in turns to shag her most energetically. Gina was very busy.

And in the back of the car she heard Darlene's voice and she glanced up at the long rear vision mirror. Darlene also had a cock in each hand, sucking each in turn. But she had stopped for a moment to speak to a man who had just arrived between her legs.

"If you want to go there, you'll have to lick me first. It needs to be properly lubricated. Condoms are in the box on the floor."

Jessica smiled and leant her head toward the open window, then she opened her mouth wide and fed that first stiff member down into her throat. With her other hand, she reached across and took hold of the other cock, running her fingers up and down to reassure it that it hadn't been forgotten.

Liquid soon surged down Jessica's throat and she smiled inside. She murmured a thank-you as the man moved away. Then she turned and smiled at the eyes above the cock she was holding, noticing as she did so that more men were lining up nearby.

One after another, penises kept coming, literally. Another surge of liquid and another happy man moved off. How many had that been, Jessica thought to herself.

As time went on, Jessica found herself thinking all sorts of crazy things. One thought was about the partner of whoever she was fucking at that moment. Who was fucking his wife, she wondered. And then who was fucking the wife of the man fucking the wife of the man fucking Jessica?

Across in the kombi, Gina's lovely legs and her high-heels where pointing skyward, held by firm hands as still another man came inside her, dropping his filled condom in the ice cream container outside the door as he withdrew and moved on, and then another pair of hands kept Gina's legs in the air and still another cock took possession of her.

In the mirror above the dashboard, Jessica looked at what Darlene was up to in the back of the van. Again, there was the vision of legs stretched upwards. But Jessica noticed with fascination that a man was stretched out beneath Darlene and his cock was firmly planted in her backside, while a second man was right up tight in her vagina and moving backwards and forwards. As if that wasn't enough, Darlene held a cock in her hand close to her mouth, sucking it with a generous amount of slurping, making noises that signalled her multiple pleasure's.

Jessica wondered if she should try fucking. So far, she had only a small amount of experience; with the young men at home and then with the two young men at the farm when she was down in the little house beside the lake with Mandy and Cindy. Then there was the three older men at The Willows retirement village.

All her experiences had been enjoyable but Jessica still didn't know if penetration could ever compare with the super wonderful feelings she felt as a result of sucking a cock.

Feeling so turned on by her sucking and looking at Gina and Darlene enjoying themselves, Jessica decided that one way or another, she would take a cock in her pussy. She first thought that the best way to do it would be to get out of the car and play it by ear, as some would say. Then she looked at the half a dozen men standing waiting for her and thought better of it.

Under some circumstance, being manhandled might be fun but this didn't seem to be the right time.

Then Jessica remembered what seemed like an obvious solution that she'd seen on the one dogging night she had attended, and decided that was the way to go.

Jessica recalled looking across at the car parked next to theirs which, on arrival, she noticed contained two women. The back right side door and the front passenger doors were open. Jessica could really only properly see the back open door and a couple of times the group of men moved so that she glimpsed the rear end of a woman kneeling on the seat. And at another moment, she glimpsed the face of a woman staring through the drivers window and seemingly doing the same thing in the front seat but on the other side of the car.

Jessica smiled through the window at the three men standing awaiting their turn and indicated to them that she was about to open the door and that she would like them to move back a little. But first she turned and knelt on the seat, facing away from the men outside. Then, when she felt comfortable and in control, Jessica turned and opened the door. The moment had arrived.

With the door open, Jessica walked herself backwards on her knees to bring her rear end level with the doorway. Her long stockinged legs below her knees stuck out of the door and her red stiletto heels were like sentries on duty that a man would need to watch out for if he was to stand between them and claim his reward. But then any man would happily risk death to own that beautiful moon shaped vision with the red suspenders and the tiny tuft of hair and the glistening pussy.

The men standing at the open door couldn't believe that what they were looking at was really on offer. The perfect bottom on perfect thighs and legs and framing a perfect pussy was a rare sight.

All around and in vehicles everywhere, there were exciting and sexy sights, large women and small ones, and in different shapes and wearing a scanty uniform that called out to onlookers to "come and try me". But Jessica rated a 10 and her admirers where in awe of her.

Then a gentlemanly voice spoke in a whisper, "You are truly beautiful. Let me introduce myself."

Jessica felt the first of what would turn out to be many entries into her vagina that day.

Occasionally a man would forget to put on a condom and would fill her with cum but before that could begin to trickle out, another solid cock would have moved in to the newly lubricated magic tunnel.

Jessica felt calm and at the same time excited. She decided she liked being fucked like this.

Dunking in the doggy position quickly became something she felt good about as well as her becoming good at it.

With interest, she noted how all those little nerve endings would celebrate more with some cocks and less with others. The sheer weight of cock numbers gave Jessica the opportunity to find out what cock activity caused the most excitement and she began to experiment, manoeuvring the inside of her cunt to bring about a better outcome.

Using her long fingers added to Jessica's enjoyment. Early on, she discovered that reaching back between her legs and touching the mens scrotums added to their enjoyment and to hers.

Sometimes she would rest the balls in her palm and jiggle them up and down. At other times, her fingers and her finger tips would surround the man's balls at the very top as though she were about to pick a pear from a branch. Another favourite was to encircle the cods at the top and pretend to milk them like the teat on a cow's udder.

Performing these movements delighted and entertained Jessica and they obviously enhanced the owners experiences too. And Jessica benefitted greatly from the mens added enthusiasm.

Darlene had mentioned how men like women to make noises and this pleased Jessica very much. She was forever wanting to sound off when she felt the need.

Sucking cock wasn't really conducive to making sounds other than wet slurpy noises. Now, as she felt each cock rocking gently or rampaging inside her, Jessica found a variety of non verbal gurgling and groaning sounds to add to the vocal expressions of her excitement, interspersing the calling out of "yes" and "harder" and "more please". And all this served to urge on the fortunate happy fellow between her legs whilst also exciting those in the line behind who could hear her.

Jessica had at last discovered that she could enjoy entertaining many cocks in the activity that they were designed for, and amidst the smell of soaps and deodorants and even the occasional whiff of cosmetics and body smells from other women, and even a hint of dry-cleaning fluid, Jessica languished in cock heaven.

The sound of the gong signalled that all activity must end in half-an-hour. A quick glance backwards told Jessica that there were still at least four men waiting and she realised that she had been on her knees accepting cocks for well over an hour. And what's more, she knew that she would be happy to accept many more.

When all was finished and the sound of car engines preparing to leave drowned out the soft background music, Gina and Darlene sat back in their own van and looked at Jessica.

"From my occasional observations, I think it would be safe to say that Jess enjoyed coming to The Dunking. What do you think, Darlene?"

"Well, she certainly didn't travel far from her front seat. And she never seemed to send a man away who wasn't satisfied. Was it okay for you, Jessica? Did you enjoy yourself?"

Jessica looked at her lady friends with a smile and with her eyes still half closed.

"Oh God, yes. I loved it. When can we come again, please?"

15

ENTERTAINING SENIORS

JESSICA WAS ASKED by Maude if she would help out with a couple of the pre Christmas musical commitments that the school had made.

The school choir leader and one of the music teachers had the bright idea that it would be good for students to perform in front of an audience to get experience. Jessica was to join two other students to visit retirement villages and give a concert during the late afternoon after residents had had their nap.

Their first gig was at The Willows, a village for wealthy retirees, situated on the coast just below Bondi. The residents loved what the students did which was a medley of songs from the 40's and 50's and everyone applauded and asked for more.

When the trio finished, the boy and girl who were a couple, downed their soft-drinks and cake and left as quickly as they could, citing another engagement further down the coast.

As Jessica finished her slice of apple cake, a couple of residents who were still at the table smiled at her and the well groomed woman with bright eyes asked Jessica if she would come to their unit for dinner the night after next. With nothing planned and not giving things much thought, Jessica agreed and when she asked what she could bring to the meal, the woman assured her that just bringing herself, would be quite sufficient.

Jessica made the short bus trip to a stop near The Willows and when she arrived, her hosts, Angela and Craig, said how very pleased they were that she had found her way there and how excited they were to see her. The unit was very beautiful and much bigger than Jessica had anticipated, boasting three bedrooms and a study as well as the lounge and a large dining alcove.

The good looking couple must have been in their mid sixty's or a little older. He was partially deaf and when his wife asked him why he wasn't wearing his hearing aids, he just answered that he couldn't find them. As a result, Craig didn't have a lot to say because he wasn't able to follow the conversation.

Jessica at first felt a little self-conscious, intending to dress more casually, she ended up confused and settled for smart conservative in a tight black skirt with a white blouse, tan stocking and standard shiny black low heels. Angela was also smartly dressed in fashionable clothes including black stockings and low heels.

The meal was excellent and Jessica enjoyed the opportunity to relax in pleasant company and enjoy a glass of wine; a white sauterne which went well with the poached fish.

When they eventually moved back into the softer light of the lounge room and sat back on the sofa and arm chairs, they swapped stories about family and their childhood upbringing and then slowly moved on to talk about their daily lives.

Craig must have realised that he was missing out on most of what was being said and rose, and excused himself, announcing that he was going in search of his missing hearing aids.

Jessica smiled at him and wished him luck, thinking what a fit and good looking couple these two older folk were.

"I would assume that an attractive young woman like yourself would have a boyfriend?" asked Angela with a knowing smile when they were suddenly alone.

Jessica laughed and replied that, no she hadn't settled on the right man or woman yet and was very happily enjoying herself and playing the field.

Angela looked happily surprised and smiled and looked at Jessica closely, then chose her words carefully.

"Can I confide in you, Jessica?"

Jessica was slightly taken aback, wondering what Angela, a mature woman, had to confide to a very young woman.

"Of course you can, Angela, but I'm not sure whether I'm a person who can be of much help. I'll soon let you know if I can or can't."

At that moment, Craig came back into the lounge room.

"Found them! Now I'm just popping up to the corner shop for more wine, darling. We're out of everything and we'll need some for tomorrow when the kids come for lunch. See you both shortly."

The two women farewelled him and Angela told him not to get lost, fixing him with a stern stare.

"I have a feeling that Craig is spending time with another woman, darling. I know I shouldn't burden you with this but I really don't have anyone outside the family or neighbours to talk to and the subject is too delicate anyway."

Angela asked Jessica to come over and join her on the sofa. Then she took Jessica's hands in hers and looked deep into her eyes.

"There's a new woman at number forty-nine. Robyn is her name. She is quite a hit with the men in the street and I'm sure some of the other wives are having the same trouble as me.

"Robyn has a woman friend visit her regularly and the two of them seem to attract the men like flies to a honey-pot. I don't know what they all get up to but it certainly keeps the men knocking on her door."

Jessica noticed that Angela had moved one of her hands onto Jessica's knee and was absentmindedly caressing it with her finger tips, as she spoke. It felt very nice. Jessica decided to take a risk.

"Have you ever been with a woman, Angela? I have a woman lover as well as male friends. I find being with a woman is emotionally very rewarding."

Angela's jaw dropped as she thought through what Jessica had just said. Then she rallied herself and with her eyes downcast, she whispered that she hadn't ever been with a woman in that way but it was something she had thought about often over the years.

Angela looked up as Jessica replied.

"I find you very attractive, Angela. Would you let me kiss you? It's all right to say no. Its just that I love everything about you. Just one kiss will do?"

Angela was flustered and didn't know where to look. She put her other hand on Jessica's thigh. Then she rallied, made the decision and looked at Jessica.

"We will have to be quick, before Craig gets home," then she closed her eyes and lent forward.

Jessica smiled and before she moved in to kiss Angela, said. "From what you have told me, I suspect your husband might enjoy seeing two women kissing.

Angela's lips touched Jessica's and the woman sat frozen in time. Then Jessica moved her lips around a little, trying to encourage Angela to participate. Then she took Angela's hand from her thigh and lifted it and put it on a breast, rotating it gently. Finally, she moved the hand on her knee up under her skirt until it touched the soft flesh above her stockings. It was then that Angela pushed her mouth against Jessica's and pushed her tongue in between Jessica's lips, making little breathless sounds indicating her excitement.

"We have lift off," Jess thought as she moved her own hand up under Angela's skirt and felt a warm spot at the top of her legs buried beneath Angela's tights.

Angela was enlivened, throwing her arms around Jessica and falling backwards and pulling the young woman on top of her. Then just as quickly, she unbuttoned her blouse, pulled out her floppy breasts from her bra and pushed Jessica's head down to suck her nipples.

"Oh Jessica this is wonderful and you are wonderful. Please keep kissing me."

"Yes, this is wonderful Angela. I'm so loving it, too."

Jessica felt Angela's hand unzipping the back of her skirt and smiled when the woman's fingers found the crack in her buttocks.

Angela's hand didn't stop there. It slid down to the back of her legs then pushed forward gently and discovering Jessica's wet pussy.

Angela sighed and pushed her lips hard against Jessica's and joined the young woman in a tongue dance. Jessica remembered that she had an urgent question for Angela and pulled her head up and looked at her.

"I do just have one important question relating to your husband, though, Angela. Tell me, do you ever suck his penis?

Jessica looked down at Angela's face which wore a look of amazement.

"Well, no I don't. My mother taught all four daughters never to touch a man there because it wasn't a nice thing to do. Strangely, whilst it's crossed my mind on occasion, I haven't had the courage to go against my mothers advice. Why do you ask?"

"It's one of the main things that women can do to keep their husbands from going elsewhere."

Jessica listened for an answer and in response to Angela's silence, except for her heavy breathing, went back to kissing her breasts while at the same time pushing her hand up hard against Angela's vagina, sheltering behind the crotch of her tights and underpants.

"I really want to taste you between your legs, Angela. I'm taking off your tights. Okay?"

"Please do, Jessica. This is all like a dream. I love it."

Jessica first removed her own skirt and then lifted Angela up and began to drag her tights down over her legs. It was when she had them down around the woman's knees, that she heard voices. It was far too late for a cover up.

Craig had brought two mates home for a drink and a supper snack and to meet their nice young visitor. He'd met the men in the street on his way home from the shops and when the men were just arriving home from golf. One was a married man who's wife happened to be away for a week, visiting one of her children. The other was a widower. All played golf together and as it happened, all visited the new woman, Robyn, at number forty-nine.

When Craig and his friends looked at what was happening on the sofa, none could believe their eyes, especially, Craig.

Angela looked up at the shocked faces of the men and found herself smiling. She had been liberated from so much in just such a short time by Jessica's loving touch, and without stopping to think, Angela called out, "We're having a party if any of you gentlemen would like to join us."

The three men stared at the two women. Angela had her breasts on show and her legs were together to facilitate her tights being removed.

"This lovely lady, gentlemen, is Jessica. As you can see, we are quite busy, but don't think you have to leave. We will happily deal with you all in a little while. Is that right Jessica? And Jessica, the good looking one in the blue trousers is Norman and the other good looking one is Matt. The other good looking one is my husband who you've already met."

Jessica turned and looked at the three well dressed and fit looking older men.

"Hello everyone. Pleased to meet you. Angela and I will certainly be happy for you to join in our fun. Why don't you all get your cocks out and warm up? We won't be too long and we are happy for you to watch."

Jessica returned to what she was doing and finished pulling off Angela's tights. Then she reached up and removed the woman's knickers, deliberately throwing them towards her husband, Craig.

Jessica now buried her head between the top of Angela's legs and licked the woman and nibbled at her clitoris. Angela sighed and closed her eyes and pushed herself up towards Jessica's face while rubbing her breasts.

Loud whispering ensued as the men excitedly talked among themselves while staring at the wondrous scene in front of them, and one by one they surrendered to Jessica's suggestion and got out their penises and began stroking them.

Jessica lifted herself up and moved up and laid on Angela and looked lovingly into the woman's smiling eyes. Angela looked back and puckered up and the two kissed.

"In a few minutes, Angela, I'm going to let you watch me suck cock. Later, you might like to forget the one piece of bad advice your mother ever gave you, and join me.

"Cock sucking is one of my favourite hobbies Angela, and it's very healthy for girl, for both the mind and her body. I won't mind if you don't suck them. You can just play with them and rub them if you like. But watch me anyway, and see what I do. Is that okay, you sexy woman?"

Angela laughed. "Sounds wonderful, Jessica. I'm desperate to learn more."

"Oh yes, there is just one more thing Angela. These gentlemen will probably want more than me sucking them and will probably want to put their cocks between both our legs.

"Are you okay with me letting Craig pop his member into me, Angela? Just say if you're not and I'll make sure he doesn't. Hopefully your Craig will soon learn the benefits of being at home with his newly liberated woman. What you do with any of other two is your call."

Angela hugged Jessica tightly then ran her hands gently over her body. "God, you sexy little bitch. I want everything. Now! And in answer to your question, do whatever you want to with Craig. I'm sure I will love watching you."

Jessica felt hands on her buttocks and experienced the thrill she always felt when touched ahead of a sexual encounter, instinctively knowing that things were about to happen. She turned her head and saw three erections standing in a row in front of the sofa. Jessica whispered to Angela that she should put her arm out and grab the nearest one and not worry about who it was attached to. Then she continued, "I'm greedy so I'll have two."

Angela giggled at Jessica's comments and immediately pushed her arm out and took a cock in her hand. Then, as Jessica moved away to sit up, Angela swung herself round to a sitting position and looked up to see who lived on the end of what she was holding, and Jessica heard an excited and breathless little voice.

"Hello Norman. You won't mind if I have a play with this, will you?"

"Well done Angela," thought Jessica. "You're on your way."

Jessica looked up at Craig who seemed confused, staring first at Jessica and then at his wife and what she was doing with Norman.

Jessica looked up at Matt, the widower, whose cock seemed the most impressive by size.

"Lovely cocks, gentlemen. I'd love to get to know them better. I hope you won't object if I do."

Jessica looked up at the two men with her sweet coy and oh-so-innocent smile. Then she a visualised a memorable scene; that moment not long ago when her first two stiff cocks presented themselves, swaying and lifting up and down beside her just outside the passenger door window at her first dogging session. And that same little voice inside Jessica screamed with delight.

Jessica reached out and took hold of Craig's cock. It instinctively jumped up and down in her hand and she fondled it lovingly.

"A girl just can't help herself at a moment like this, Craig. I might get carried away and lick and suck you both. Is that okay? Tell me to stop if you want."

As she spoke her words caused the two cocks to jump upwards. With her other hand Jessica took hold of Matt and she began a slow rubbing motion on the two of them.

Jessica played with her two cocks for a just a few moments rubbing her fingers over their hoods and tickling their testicles, then one after the other she took turns feeding them in between her lips and slowly licking and sucking them. Jessica chanced a look over at Angela and discovered that the woman had indeed watched Jessica and was now busily sucking Norman whose face showed a level of ecstasy that Jessica hadn't seen in a man for a long time.

Angela looked as though she was truly enjoying herself and Jessica recalled the first time that she and Edith and Rosa had laid on the bed in a cool room on a hot summers day and discovered one another, and how the world had been the better for it ever since.

Jessica was loving having access to cocks again. It had only been a couple of weeks since her wonderful sex filled holiday at Goulburn but she still felt as though she hadn't had a proper cock for in ages.

Jessica had still to experience being fucked and enjoying it with as much pleasure as her sucking provided. But she did like it and was aware that fucking was what men ultimately felt was their reason for being. For that reason she considered it important to make it available to them. It was important for her not to be selfish.

Encouraging men to have their way was a form of insurance. Being certain that they would be happy to be sucked again was assured when they knew they would be the beneficiaries of a full service afterwards.

Jessica remembered that thing that Gina had said the evening they were dogging in Goulburn. "I'm going to open the door on the other side shortly. I need to offer my other end. The boys deserve the full menu."

After quite sometime in cock play, Jessica decided it was time to move on to fucking mode. But before she did, she wanted to do one thing.

"Angela? Can I have a turn with Norman please? Lets swap places. Angela nodded her agreement without letting go of Norman's cock and Jessica stood up and walked around the back of her two men and behind Norman, and Angela moved over. Within moments, Angela had a two cocks to deal with, one being her husbands. Without missing a beat, she smiled up at Craig and Matt and took turns feeding them into her mouth, slurping generously on both of them.

Around ten or fifteen minutes after the change over, Jessica whispered as best she could to Angela that she was about to get onto her knees and show the boys what she was offering next on the menu. Angela almost choked laughing. "I'll watch and then I might do the same," she replied.

Jessica stopped sucking Norman and looked up at him.

"I fancy you in a different spot now, Norman. Hope you will be happy with it."

Then Jessica stood and turned around and knelt on the sofa, displaying her backside and vagina.

All the men looked at Jessica's rear end, and as they did so, Angela took the opportunity to do what Jessica had just done. She turned and perched on the edge of the sofa on her knees. Jessica noticed and instructed the men accordingly.

"We are offering unrestricted access here today. Please enjoy yourselves, gentlemen. We certainly will."

There was a sudden rush. Three cocks and only two pussies.

Craig plunged his member into his wife without further ado and Norman took a slow easy approach to pussy poking at Jessica's already wet rear end.

Angela kindly called to Matt to come and sit beside her so that she could rub and play with him to which he acted swiftly, accepting her kind offer.

Having her husband shagging her, excited Angela for some reason she couldn't quite understand. Was it to do with her sudden arrival into a world of more honest interactions. Was him fucking her in this situation like what it was going to be for them both from now on. Was she conscious that this was likely to be the successful way of weaning him away from that tart up the road? She did love him, and hoped all of these things were true. Then she smiled to herself and the new Angela thought how nice it would be to fuck his two friends before the night was over. Other mens cocks were probably the last essential ingredient in her liberation.

Jessica had considered the lack of condoms but dismissed it as a concern, telling herself that these men were probably clean and she had been for a check-up this week and was fine.

Funny how we tell ourselves reassuring things when it suits us, she mused.

Craig came quite quickly and Angela felt a huge load slipping around in her and she also experienced small orgasmic tremors in her genitals. He bellowed like a bull and everyone smiled.

As her husband left her, she looked up and smiled and blew him a kiss. Then she turned to Matt.

"I'd would love it if you fucked me too, Matt. But only if you want to."

Matt was up and at her in just moments, and Craig turned and watched in awe.

"Oh, Matt, how kind of you. Give it to me like it's your last one ever, Matt, and I'll make you your favourite chocolate cake tomorrow."

What more of an incentive could a man ask for, Jessica smiled to herself, overhearing Angela's offer. Then she thought about not having made a chocolate cake for ages and that she, being the top cake maker of her final school year, should surprise Edith with one next week.

Norman came with a bleating sound accompanied by what sounded like a last gasp.

"Thank you Norman. Craig? You've given it all to that other slut. But perhaps you could manage to give me a little touch up, please?"

Craig stepped forward and put his hand between Jessica's legs and fingered her very wet pussy. She returned the favour by gently rubbing his balls. Then she took his hand in hers and pushed three of his fingers into her vagina really hard and moved them vigorously, in and out. Then Jessica uttered a little scream and came on Craig's hand.

"Thank you Craig. Just what I needed."

The men stood or sat around, a little dazed and unsure of themselves, like boys thinking they were still about to get into trouble for what they had been doing. But then Angela put her arms around her husband who sat on the floor in front of her, and nibbled his ear.

"Thank you darling. What a wonderful husband you are. Hope you liked it. Just ask when you want some more."

Jessica laughed and looked at the other two men and said how she thought that they were pretty good too.

There wasn't a lot to chat about at that moment, so Jessica thought she should say something.

"Thank you all. I really enjoyed your company tonight and want to thank Angela for making it possible. At the risk of looking stupid, would you raise your hands if you feel you would like to do it all again sometime. If Angela and Craig were willing of course, I'd happily come over to their house again for another romp."

Everyone put their hand up then Jessica looked at Angela.

"I look forward to hearing from you, Angela."

When the men had shuffled off home, or in Craig's case, farewelling Jessica and excused himself and headed off to bed, the two women reached out for each other and kissed then rolled onto the sofa together.

"Oh my God, Jessica. Life will never be the same again, thanks to you."

Jessica moved quickly, put her head down between Angela's legs and began to slurp up what two lovely men had left behind and was now dribbling from her new love. This was nectar to the extraordinary cock loving Jessica. Then just as she was finishing and about to take her mouth away, she felt Angela stiffen and realised that the woman's pussy was looking for more.

With three deft fingers and a thumb, Jessica gave Angela her first proper orgasm in a long time, enjoying the moment when Angela arched her back and screamed out. Then she held her in her arms while the newly liberated lovely lady sobbed and placed sloppy kisses all over any part of Jessica she could reach.

The two settled down and rested in each others arms.

"Angela?"

"Yes, Jessica?"

"Did you like sucking cock, darling?"

"Loved it!"

"And being fucked by other cocks?"

"Loved it!"

16

SWINGING IN RETIREMENT

JESSICA VISITED HER NEW FRIENDS, Angela and husband Craig, every six or eight week at their unit at The Willows, a retirement village for well off retirees. It wasn't that she wouldn't have liked to see more of them, it was to do with the amount of time available to her, what with study and her other activities.

Enjoying herself at Angela's place was most enjoyable for the good food and company as well as the sex with neighbours, usually the same two men plus Craig.

Jessica was Angela's first female sex partner and her coming out and her liberation meant that she was keen to catch up on those things in life that she thought she had missed out on. So when Angela called her and asked her if she was up for a visit and something a little different, Jessica jumped at the opportunity.

"I hope its still rude, whatever it is, Angela?" Jessica asked, laughingly.

"Definitely!" Angela assured her.

"Are you going to give me a hint, at least, you senior slut?"

Angela laughed. She loved it when Jessica called her a senior slut. It sounded like she was the holder of an important position in life. And Jessica assured her that indeed, it was very important.

"If I said there would be a lot more cocks and probably extra women, would that interest you, my little baby slut?"

Jessica was immediately excited and screamed her answer into the telephone.

"God yes, Angela. I'm looking for my lubricant as we speak. Are the ladies experienced, can I ask, or do we have to introduce them to the better things of life."

Angela screamed back her amusement.

"Well, Jessica, it seems that, unknown to me, there are quite a number of swinging residents here at the village and also among other members of Craig's golfing fraternity. He says there are at least half a dozen bringing their partners who will no doubt be expecting to have a good time with other womens husbands.

"Robyn, our honeypot from number 49 wants to join us. She's already visited me during an afternoon when Craig was at golf. If I just tell you that we got on famously, you will get the picture."

Jessica feigned disapproval.

"You slut, you. Do I have to share you now with an experienced bisexual superstar who lives practically on the premises? How will I ever be able to compete?"

"Oh you are a darling. I think you will like her. And if you don't, well you can fight it out between sucking and fucking all the men and women that are coming. Half the golf club apparently, if Craig isn't exaggerating."

"Well, bitch. I'll certainly be there to compete for cocks with the two of you. So watch out!"

Jessica made a point of being late. It wasn't something she would normally do but there was method in her madness. She knew that making a late entrance would get her the most attention and dressed in her sluttiest clothes, she knew she would get an interesting reception.

Strangely, it wasn't the men she wanted to impress the most, it was the honeypot woman, Robyn. If it came to a cock sucking stand-off, Jessica wanted to win. Then she reminded herself that she was being foolish; but then reminded herself again that she was going there to have fun and there was nothing worth fighting over.

Angela and Craig's apartment was crowded. Everyone was still going through the niceties of greeting each other and asking after each others health. But a few that had got there early and had a couple of glass's of wine, were already showing signs of wanting to try out with someone.

Jessica found Angela and they kissed and then Angela took her and introduced her to Robyn who immediately put an arm around Jessica's waist and pulled her close. Then she kissed her on the lips saying how Angela had told her all about her tall young friend. But there was too much going on and too much noise for anyone to have a proper conversation.

Jessica told her host that she would like to have a little wander about on her own to get the feel of things and Angela smiled and replied that the sooner people started feeling things, the better.

Handsome well dressed men and women were everywhere and Jessica thought how much they reminded her of the crowd at the dunking she had been to with Gina and Darlene.

Not everyone was in the same mould, however. In the kitchen she discovered a huge blond woman in a brightly floral kaftan and with bare feet, wearing her hair braided like she had just got off the plane from Bali.

She wore blue eyeshadow and pink lipstick and her varnished finger and toe nails were pink. She spoke with a Dutch accent and threw her arms around any man that came within touching distance, kissing him passionately and telling him with only a slight slur in her guttural accented voice, that she hoped he would favour her body before the night was out. They each murmured something which Jessica couldn't catch accept the woman's name sounded like Dunya.

"Well, that will be interesting," thought Jessica, looking at the woman. She would surely have been six-foot three or four and had a huge backside and enormous breasts.

In the passageway that led to the toilet, a couple where in each others arms and kissing passionately. In the lounge, men and women were talking and laughing and quite a few men and some women were rubbing someones rear end, affectionately, a preliminary signalling perhaps.

It wasn't until she looked into the first of the dimly lit bedrooms that she saw things we're really starting to get under way.

A good looking well built man was leaning against a wardrobe door with his trousers and pants down around his ankles. Two women knelt in front of him sucking what looked to be a sizeable and happy cock, and passing it backwards and forwards to each other. One woman had a hand between the others legs who in turn was slowly unbuttoning the shirt of the woman feeling her up. Jessica's response was to put her own hand down and slide her fingers up under her mini skirt. She would have liked to join in but thought she would keep looking around before making any moves.

As she turned to leave the room, a smiling woman entered followed closely by two men. The woman had a cock in each hand and headed to the double bed. Then she stopped and let their cocks go while she lifted her dress up over her head and then unfastened her bra and let it drop to the floor. Then Jessica heard the woman speak in a low sensuous voice, "Who wants to be first?"

Jessica couldn't help but feel horny. But she was determined to have a good look around. She still had two bedrooms to look in plus the dining room.

In the second bedroom, at first she thought it was empty, but then she heard sounds coming from the carpeted floor on the other side of the bed and tippy-toed across and peeped.

She was surprised but enchanted with the hot scene that confronted her, and what was being said was even more exciting.

A woman was on her knees with her bare bum in the air. A second woman wearing a dildo was shagging her vagina energetically, and talking in a breathless voice, "I know you've been fucking him for ages, you bitch. But all along, it was me that you were after, wasn't it? Wasn't it? Bitch? Well, now you've go me and I'll expect more of this, you dirty little husband fucker. From now on you will come to my place once a week and get what I'm giving you now. And you are going to have to fuck me too. Have you got that, slut?"

A weak sobbing voice answered. "Yes, yes, Susan. Oh yes. Just keep shagging me, Susan. Please don't stop. I want it."

Jessica was rubbing herself furiously, wanting to be both the fucker and the fuckee. She made a mental note of the two women in case she ran across them again later.

Bedroom three, and what a scene. Two men were holding a women up off the floor, each with a shapely leg over their respective arms. Her arms held each man around the neck. All her clothing had been removed except for her stockings and suspender belt. A third man was fucking her enthusiastically, yelling that he was about to come. The woman screamed her satisfaction then let herself down from the two men while they changed places and the next man fucked her equally enthusiastically. Jessica figured that the woman had probably already had the third man before Jessica arrived.

When this third man finished, the woman let herself down, bent down and picked up her clothes and, without looking at anyone, mumbled something like thanks fellas and walked out.

Jessica saw the same woman a little later in the dining alcove on her hands and knees while three men took turns at her from the rear. And jumping ahead, in the early hours of the morning, when Jessica was being had from behind by a big happy man, the same woman put her head in the door and spoke. "Will you be long Gary? I'd like to go. I'm quite tired and ready for bed."

Such was the world of experienced swingers, apparently, and for some reason, Jessica thought about that moment a lot over the coming weeks.

———

Jessica wandered off out of the laundry, leaving Angela and Sally planning their next adventure.

As she was passing by the double doors that led to the little dining area and sun room, she glanced in and saw three men sitting on a sofa. They looked much older than the other men she'd seen so far. They were happily laughing and talking and Jessica thought how relaxed they were and she wanted to know more about them.

"Hello gentlemen. Can I join you?" she ventured as she came close and they looked up at her.

Jessica put them all in their late seventies and thought how she had never seen three men this age together before. They seemed so relaxed and unthreatening and she wanted to know them better.

Three sets of appreciative and smiling eyes stared at Jessica.

"Welcome to the gang of three, dearest lady. You are very beautiful. Please come and sit with us. Move up Henry and let the girl have a seat. That is Colin up that end, Henry in the middle and I'm John. What is your name?"

"I'm Jessica. Pleased to meet you all."

Jessica squeezed in between Henry and John.

"How is it that three fine looking men like you are all alone. Have you finished with all the lovely woman here already? Or have you been told to behave yourselves?"

The three men laughed and John answered. "Well, Jessica. We are all in our mid eighties but we have one other thing in common. All three of us have wives who are much younger than us and as you can imagine, because of our age, the girls are missing out on some of the things we were once keen to share with them. As a result, we like to bring them somewhere where they can meet younger men and get a bit of you-know-what. This means that we can all stay happily married."

Then Colin added his voice to the conversation. "We can get them up but they're just not hard enough anymore, are they boys.

"We love our wives so we are happy that they can get a good stiff cock in them at do's like this. My Mary came past a few minutes ago to see if we were okay and said all three were having a great time and their only worry was that they might be running out of cocks."

John laughed and said how if that was the case, his Maureen would want him to put on the dildo when they got home and he wouldn't get to sleep until the early hours.

Jessica was fascinated by what these jolly men were saying. She wondered if the three men's wives gave their cocks any attention but decided not to ask.

Jessica decided to play the innocent girl. Well, sort of innocent.

She told the three gentlemen about how difficult it was to find men who would just give her a gentle touch up and play with her breasts and caress her and talk to her. As she did so, she put a hand on John and Henry's knees and lightly rubbed them.

"That sounds about all we can do, girl. Would you like us to play with you then? We certainly won't hurt you. Why don't you lay yourself across our legs so that we can all have a bit of you. Do that and we'll see how we go. What do you think fella's.

A thrill ran through Jessica's body. She stood up and surveyed the men, then she lifted the hem of her skirt and asked them if she should she lay face up or face down. Two out of three said face down, so the excited girl carefully laid on top of six legs, her shoes touching the arm of the sofa one end her head on John's trousers at the other end.

"That is nice, isn't it fellas? She's quite something isn't she? Look at those legs."

Jessica felt six sets of fingers moving gently up and down on the back of her legs.

"I bet she's got a nice little bum up here somewhere, too."

Jessica felt someone unzipping her skirt and she lifted herself a little bit and put her hand underneath to show them and help whoever it was, wanting to pull the skirt down.

"May as well take it right off, Col."

With her skirt gone, Jessica felt hands on her bottom.

"Take her knickers off, too, Col."

Jessica smiled to herself, knowing three sets of eyes were feasting on her bare backside. Then she felt a finger on her little anus, going round and round but not intruding.

"Nice little Poppy's parlour", came the voice of Henry.

"How come you call it that, Henry. Never heard it before."

Jessica felt wonderful. Fingers played gently with her ankles and moved her shoes on and off her feet. She wondered if Collin had a foot or shoe fetish and when he alternated between her two feet, she figured that he had both. She loved it.

"When I was a youngster living in a village in England, the youngest of the girls who lived a couple of doors up from us was named Poppy. You don't hear it these days. I quite liked it and I liked her.

She was a happy girl but some folk thought she wasn't all there, so to speak. She seemed vague at times and you could never be sure what she was thinking or what she would do next. She wasn't subnormal or anything, though some called her one of gods Angels which in those days usually meant mentally handicapped."

Jessica felt John's hands slide under the top of her body and slide beneath her blouse and find her nipples. This was bliss, she thought.

"When I was much older, my mother told me that Poppy's mum, Ivy Gateshead, told my mum something she had told her daughter when she was fourteen.

"She told the young Poppy that as she got older, men would start to give her a lot of attention and that she had to be especially careful what she did with men or they might get her pregnant. She told her that what she had between her legs was called the bedroom, and what she had between the cheeks of her bum was called the parlour. She went on to tell Poppy that she must never let any boy put his willy in her bedroom, and she could only let him into the parlour, just like when they had special visitors at home.

"She told her that one day. when Poppy had a husband, she could let him into the bedroom so that they would be able to make babies."

Jessica thought what a lovely story this was and with all the attention her body was getting from the three mens fingers, she felt that she would happily be the mens Poppy and let any of them into her parlour.

"Poppy developed early and her breasts attracted a lot of attention which excited her. Being so innocent and not wanting to offend, she discovered that by letting boys, and later, men into her parlour, she was suddenly much admired and loved by all. She also discovered that she really liked having someone visit in the parlour and it wasn't long before Poppy's parlour was a euphemism in the village for any girls back entrance."

Jessica was loving this story so much. Then she noticed movement beneath her. It was in John's trousers. He was obviously aroused and she couldn't be sure if it was a reaction to touching her or to his story. She figured it was both.

"What a great story, John. I take it you made visits to the parlour?"

"I did Henry. I was a bit younger than Poppy, but when I was eighteen and she was probably nineteen, I was out walking near the Oak forest just a mile from the village, with my friend, Bernard, when we ran into Polly. She smiled her dreamy far-away-look smile at us then she said she wanted to show us something.

"Poppy led us off the track into the woods a short distance. Then she turned and unbuttoned our trousers and took out our cocks and rubbed and sucked them.

"This was all new to us and very exciting. Then she pulled up her skirt and pulled off her knickers and knelt down on the soft leaves, displaying her backside. Then she looked up at us and said that we had to take turns in putting our cocks into her parlour. She pulled the cheeks of her bum apart and showed us where to put them.

"After a bit of confusion and with Poppy's help, we managed to get into her and happily rode the lady, listening to her moan and groan as though she was unhappy, but when we enquired after her wellbeing she informed us that she was very happy and if we were happy, then we should keep putting our willies in her parlour.

"Over the years Poppy got a reputation and there came a time when there was hardly a man in the village, young or old, who hadn't visited Polly's parlour.

"Then one day she met a young man and they fell in love and got married and she went on to give birth to eight beautiful children.

"A was in my twenties and I accompanied my mother too the wedding. I will always remember her dabbing her eyes as we watched the bride and groom leave the church, and saying, 'She's the only girl in the village that deserves to wear white.'"

Jessica could feel the large bump in Johns trousers getting bigger which excited her, and she began to unbutton his fly. She soon had his respectable cock in her hand and shortly after that, in her mouth.

Then with a spare hand, she reached down to where Henry also had a lump in his trousers and Jessica signalled to him that she wanted him to expose his member. Then she rubbed her knee against Colin's crotch and felt movement in his trousers.

Jessica swung herself off the men and kneeled on the floor, sucking John and rubbing Henry. Then Jessica moved to suck Henry leaving both hands free to rub Colin's newly liberated cock while continuing to rub John's.

"By jove, this girl has got what it takes. I think I'm actually going to be able to give her something."

John was about to erupt and Jessica managed to get him into her mouth the moment before it happened.

Just as she was swallowing John's present, Henry began to tremble in that way Jessica knew pre-empted a man's orgasm and she got his contribution without loosing a drop.

As the first two men slumped back and smiled through dreamy eyes at their beautiful liberator, Colin spurted forth into Jessica's loving mouth, then slumped backward alongside the other two.

"What an amazing woman you are, Jessica. I'm sure I can speak for all of us when I say thank you and extend to you our very best wishes," said John, affectionately.

Jessica stood and looked down upon them, regretting it was all over. She felt she could have let them touch and play with her forever.

"Thank you gentlemen. I really enjoyed your company. Can a girl be a bit forward and ask if you would like to see here again and if so, where she might find you all? I loved getting your attention and I would be happy to be your Poppy and let you visit her parlour, and now, thanks to the contraceptive pill, she could even let you into the bedroom.

"I just love being with you any which way. And sucking you all was a bonus. Are you ever available? Unfortunately I'm at work during the day so it would have to be in the evenings or at the weekends."

The men rallied themselves and looked at each other and nodded. Then John rallied himself.

"Our wives go to the swingers club together on the second Monday night of each month. They get home very late. At around 2 am, usually. We three usually get together for a drink and supper and watch TV or play cards.

"I believe I can safely say that we would much prefer to watch and play with you, Jessica. You could come over after eight o'clock to 89 Seaview Crescent, The Willows. We would love to see you."

17

A MOST MEMORABLE NIGHT

Jessica was surprised when a call came through one evening from Robyn, the woman her friend Angela called the Honeypot.

Jessica had met Robyn at Angela's swingers night at The Willows retirement village a month or more back. All three women had had a very enjoyable night, both with the lots of horny people who came along and also with each other.

"Hello Robyn. Nice to hear from you. How can I help?"

Jessica listened as Robyn giggled and spluttered and mumbled before answering coherently.

"Well, darling girl. I'm organising a night which I thought you might be interested in attending. It is free to you as I will enjoy having you there as will everyone else, I'm sure.

I've had an evening like this before and I thoroughly enjoyed myself. Actually, it is the niece of a friend who organises things. Sharna works in the admin section at one of the universities. She is a bit older than you, around her late twenties I expect.

"To be brief, the event is really a gang-bang or perhaps a better labeled would be a cock fest, but a clean and friendly one.

"Shana chooses and enlists students who she judges as suitable for the job. She organises a venue quite close to the university, and we simply show up and show ourselves off. The lads do the rest. I pay her a small amount to defray costs and depending on the number of students she's getting in.

"The arrangement naturally includes her in the event. Shana is a very sexual woman and loves to get a go at all the lads.

"So darling, what do you think? I've put in an order for fourteen young men to share between the three of us. If you enjoy it, we could always do it again and get more lads if needs be."

Jessica was a little taken aback by Robyn's offer. She didn't know the woman very well. But then they had enjoyed each other very much on the bedroom carpet with Angela later in the evening when they all accepted that they had run out of cocks for the night. Yes, the Honeypot was fun.

"So kind of you to ask me, Robyn, and yes, I will be most happy to accompany you to this exciting event. Text me the details when you're ready."

Jessica was about to hang up, but suddenly thought about something she needed advice about.

"Robyn? Before you go. What should girl wear to something like this?"

More laughter from the other end.

"Well whatever you wear darling, I can guarantee that it won't be on you for very long.

"You looked beautiful and sexy at Angela's swingers night. I so loved your cummerbund suspender belt darling and I'm sure everyone else did too. And lads these days are all looking at porn on the web and most of the women are still wearing what I wear, traditional lingerie, a corselet, a bra, panties, stockings and heels.

"Stick to what you feel good in, darling and you can't go wrong."

Jessica went to bed and dreamed of having many stiff cocks all chasing her down to the little hut beside the lake at the farm near Goulburn where she had enjoyed a wonderful holiday. When she got inside the hut in her dream, she threw herself on the mattress and let them all jump all over her.

Jessica wasn't sure that she had the right address as she stared at the old brick warehouse in a backstreet in the inner Sydney suburb of Surry Hills. Then she saw a door open further along the lane and a group of people entered and she headed towards it. A dim yellow light illuminated the door and Jessica pressed the door bell.

A very attractive young woman in a tight shirt and skirt and very high heels greeted her and introduced herself as Sharna and ushered Jessica through a narrow hallway into a small sparsely furnished room full of smiling young men who hooted and catcalled on seeing the leggy Jessica come into view.

"That's enough fellas. Behave please. Show some respect. This is Jessica who looks forward to meeting you all soon. The show doesn't start until you are all here and at the moment there are still two of you missing. Knock on the door when they arrive.

Shana took Jessica's hand and led her down a short passage and through a door into a small sitting room.

"Is Robyn here yet, Sharna?"

Sharna smiled and explained that Robyn had phoned the day before to say she wouldn't make it. She had told Shana that she foolishly went to a surprise swinger event in her street. She said how good it was because there were many more men than women and as a result, she received a lot of attention. This led to her being exceedingly sore the next day and she realised she would have to do without tonights entertainment.

She said she wouldn't call you because you might decided not come and she didn't want you to miss the fun.

"So how many men are coming, Sharna? Can we manage them all between the two of us?

Sharna smiled at Jessica and put a hand out and touched her cheek.

"You are very beautiful, Jessica. Any chance that I will get to kiss you later? Is it something you would do?"

Jessica reached out and put a hand on Sharna's chest and smiled.

"I'd like to kiss you right now, Sharna. May I?"

At that moment, a side door opened and an older woman came in. She smiled a big happy smile.

"This must be Jessica? What a gorgeous young thing. Competing with you two is going to be difficult but I'll settle for a bit less."

Jessica smiled at the attractive solidly built older woman.

"Jessica, this is Robyn's friend and my aunt, Crystal. She volunteered to help out when she heard that Robyn couldn't get here.

"Crystal? I'm just about to kiss Jessica. I'm sure she would be happy to let you have one too."

Jessica laughed and replied that some attention from both of the women would be welcomed.

Sharna unbuttoned Jessica's blouse and then she and Crystal put their arms around Jessica and took turns kissing her mouth and her breasts while both women slipped their hands up Jessica's short skirt and discovered her already wet little pussy and played with it.

Jessica hungrily put a hand up each of the womens skirts to lovingly palm their warm moist hairy vaginas. Crystal's curvaceousness ensured that her skirt was very tight and Jessica's hand became trapped between the woman's thighs.

"Are you looking forward to all those cocks out there, darling?" Sharna murmured.

"Oh yes, Sharna. It is my first time but I think I'll manage. How many will there be?"

"Well it was to be around sixteen but it's now down to fourteen. I hope that will be enough."

All three women laughed and Crystal joked that she would need at least eight of those, "So bad luck to you two".

"Now, Jessica. Make sure you assert yourself when necessary. The lads all know that no means no. And it is understood that you can push a hand away if it is annoying you. This usually only happens when an overzealous fellow wants to maul your pussy or it could be that he is doing something that you are not happy about.

"Another thing I should mention is that I've instructed the young men that there is to be no coming on faces. I told them to simply remember the four b's - breasts, belly, back and butt and unless invited, not to cum anywhere else.

"Now I forgot to check with Robyn what your feelings were about anal? Are you okay with it or not."

Jessica was writhing under the delicious feelings she was getting from the womens' attention and she couldn't help thinking of her dogging guru Gina talking about warming up. Jessica was definitely warming up. She managed to gasp her answer.

"I'm fine with anal, thanks for asking."

There was a knock on the door and a voice called out, "Ready when you are, Sharna."

"I'll just say before we go in, these lads are mostly in their early to mid twenties. From what I know about them, they are usually a polite and caring group, but we know that men can change when confronted with erotic situations and might well act a little differently. I'm confident though, that whatever they get up to, we'll be able to handle it."

The three women stopped feeling each other up and laughed. Then the bright eyed and elegantly dressed older Crystal spoke. "Lets go and handle it now. I'm more than ready. But I doubt well get a five tonight but I'm happy with a four."

Jessica asked what she meant.

"One in each hand, one to suck and two between the legs is a five. These lads might be too innocent to make it a five."

The three laughed and Jessica thought how good this all seemed.

"With a bit of luck I'll get the lads who desperately want to fuck an experienced full-figured older woman. I can usually pick them. You'd be amazed what I can get in return for the phrase 'come aboard your first ocean cruiser …'"

Then Sharna went and got a squeegee bottle from a cupboard.

"Hang on a moment girls. Lift your skirts and pull down your pants and let me squeeze some lubricant into your butts.

"And Jessica, just remember that you are in charge of everything even if you think you're not.

Sharna moved towards the door.

"Give me just a moment while I organise them. I'll knock when they're ready."

Sharna knocked on the door and led the two others along a passageway to a large dimly lit room. It was warm and comfortable. Three padded divan's bases were lined up in the middle of the room and fourteen naked young men stood against the wall, most with their hands over their cocks.

Sharna gestured to Jessica to take the far end bed and Crystal to take the middle one. Then Sharna introduced the women by name adding that all were excited to be there to meet the boys. Then she invited them to stroll around and "get to know us". "And don't be shy. We all know why we are here. Lets enjoy ourselves."

Jessica couldn't help but feel excited but also nervous. She recalled Gina's wonderful attitude when dealing with the men on their dogging expedition and how she personalised each and every encounter with the men that presented themselves to her. Jessica wanted to be like Gina, but was it possible in this situation?

Jessica kneeled on the bed and spread her hands over the front of her frock and moved them around on her breasts. Suddenly there were two, then three then four men standing beside the bed and she knew that she was required to make the next move.

Jessica could see three cocks pointing in her direction. She put her hand out and took hold of just one and looked up at the face that owned it.

"Hello! What's your name?"

A slightly embarrassed face looked down at Jessica.

"I'm Douglas."

"Hello Douglas. I'm Jessica. Pleased to meet you."

Introductions over, Jessica took Douglas's cock into her mouth and began to lick and suck him, at the same time thinking that this was a most civilised way of doing the thing she loved most. But then things got even better.

Fingers touched an ankle and started to climb up the back of her right leg. Then Jessica felt other fingers, this time on her left leg and behind her knee and they too were on a slow march upwards. Then the hands of a third party lifted her skirt up over her back and Jessica felt palms on each buttock. And as this was happening, a second cock was jostling for position with Douglas's, anxiously searching for her response. Jessica kept sucking but stopped touching Douglas's balls and took the second cock in hand.

Douglas reached a hand forward and slipped it inside the top of Jessica's top and inside her bra and fondled her lovingly.

Jessica removed Douglas's cock and looked up at him.

"Do you want to cum now or later, Douglas?"

"Now, please."

Jessica increased pressure with her hand and with her lips and mouth and in no time at all, Douglas shot his load down her throat.

Jessica looked up and smiled and nodded a 'thank you' then turned and looked up at who was on the end of her second cock.

"Hello! What's your name?"

A cheerful face looked down at Jessica.

"I'm John."

"Hello John. I'm Jessica. Pleased to meet you."

Jessica took John's cock into her mouth and began to suck him.

The activity at her rear was hotting up in more ways than one and Jessica realised that her skirt had been unzipped and was about to be dragged off over her shoes and her panties were moving down over her stockinged legs close behind, and again Jessica couldn't help but recall Gina's words, "A girl is not dogging until she removes her knickers."

Jessica was suddenly alerted to John's early ejaculation as he poured his contribution into her. As John moved away he was immediately replaced with another person offering a stiff erection, waving it in front of Jessica's happy face.

"Hello! What's your name?"

A nervous looking lad with glasses looked down at Jessica.

"I'm Scot."

"Hello Scot. I'm Jessica. Pleased to meet you."

Introductions over, Jessica took Scots's cock into her mouth and began to suck him.

Jessica closed here eyes, savouring the moment. She couldn't count the number of hands and fingers feasting on her rear and all she knew was that the feeling was exquisite. Her top had been unbuttoned and she moved her arms to let the liberator remove it. Apart from her shoes and stockings and garter belt, Jessica was naked and she luxuriated in that wonderful moment.

Enjoying the nervous Scot's cock along with the delicious rear action, Jessica took a moment off to glance across and listen to what was happening next door to her. Crystal was on her back with her shapely solid legs pointing to the ceiling and her feet pirouetting with excitement. A young man was energetically exercising her pussy.

Scot yelled and deposited his contribution down Jessica's throat and immediately he moved away, a new penis arrived at the gate.

Jessica's eyes were momentarily closed as she rejoiced in the man-handling she was receiving at the rear. A hand was rubbing her pussy and was immediately followed by a wet sloppy mouth kissing and licking her.

"Hello! What's your name?"

A very happy looking young man with a swarthy look smiled down at the still closed eyes on Jessica's face.

"I'm Brad."

"Hello Brad. I'm Jessica. Pleased to meet you."

Jessica opened her eyes and looked up at the man and couldn't help but be uplifted by his strong looks and his smile. Then she lowered her gaze to look at his cock and was transfixed. Brad's member was very big and healthy and sat in a bush of curly hair. She felt as though he were presenting her with a posy of flowers.

Jessica didn't immediately put him in her mouth but instead, stuck out her tongue and circled the tip of Brad's cock in a slow loving movement. This was partly to savour the delights of his member plus she wanted to be able to talk to Brad and if she had managed to get him into her mouth, she would be tongue tied.

"Are you from Sydney, Brad?"

"No, Goulburn, or rather just past Goulburn. The folks have a farm there."

Jessica was intrigued. "I have friends just the other side of Goulburn, Brad. They have a property, Muta East. Do you know it?"

Jessica was now rubbing Brad's cock and noting how solid it was.

"Our neighbours! I do a bit of work for Brendan and Bella. Wonderful couple and really good property managers. Good friends of mum and dad too."

Jessica was trying hard to concentrate on what Brad was saying. She desperately wanted to know more about him but their was someone attempting to enter her at the back making things a little tricky. Jessica gave a gasp has her suitor finally made his entry, then he settled in to a quiet slow shagging mode which afforded her the opportunity to ask another question.

"What is your surname, Brad. I'll mention I met you but not where I met you."

The two laughed.

"It's Braithwaite and it's probably better that you don't, although to be honest, it wouldn't much matter. Bernie and Mildred are very broad minded. In fact they are members of the same swingers group as Bren and Bella. But I've been in Sydney for a month doing a course and I wouldn't want them thinking I was having too good a time."

Jessica knew that she was running out of time. Things at the back were picking up speed and she couldn't really keep Brad in conversation, especially when he was just out having a good time, although Brad seemed more than happy just to talk. Then Jessica remembered something.

"When I was there, I noticed there was a dogging night at the cemetery. Do you go to that Brad or are you too young?"

"Mum and dad go sometimes, although mum's been crook for a while so I don't think she's been lately. Yes. I'm too young. But that's okay. Us younger set have our own fun at the same cemetery on a Friday night and I sometimes go to that.

"I'll tell you what. The next time you are over my way and you feel like a fun night out, give me a call. I'll come and pick you up."

Jessica felt more excited at Brad's invitation than she had been about anything else in recent times. Now she had to cement the friendship.

"Thanks Brad. I'll try and get there for the next holiday fortnight. Now I better check you out properly."

Jessica launched on the most heart-felt sucking episode of her life. She carefully managed to get Brad's enormous cock into her mouth before setting out on a very loving voyage. But it was not a long voyage. Brad stroked Jessica's hair and touched her forehead then removed himself from her mouth.

"Are you moving to the back end, Brad, just as I was really enjoying you here?"

Brad laughed and bent and kissed Jessica's cheek.

"Sorry, Jessica. I've gotta go. I promised Shana that I'd be her fantasy man, Brad the very bad cousin, her 'bastard from the bush' as she wants to call me.

"Make sure you call when you next get to Goulburn."

Jessica would have been devastated at Brad leaving if it wasn't for what was now happening in her pussy and for the fingers gently tugging her nipples. So much was happening and she was loving it, and then there was a new cock waving in front of her face.

"Hello! What's your name?"

A grinning plumpish young man smiled down at her.

"I'm Linton."

"Hello Linton. I'm Jessica. Pleased to meet you."

Linton was a lucky boy. Jessica managed to erase the image of Brad by giving the blow job she'd planned for him, to Linton.

Then Jessica felt her body being lifted and rolled over so that she lay back and across the bed.

She quickly looked down between her legs and saw that three keen cocks were standing to attention, seemingly looking forward to getting into her now very wet vagina. Her legs were quickly lifted into the air at the same moment as one of the cocks rammed into her. She lifted herself to meet him and to give herself and him that little extra pleasure from his energetic ramming.

Jessica put Linton back in her mouth then reached out to two more cocks standing each side of her. In her mind she registered that she was now enjoying a four pointer.

On the next bed, Crystal was kneeling and venting her older-woman wrath on the lad attacking her from the back. On either side of him, two lads were holding Crystal's ankles to prevent her moving away and her significant objects of desire were well and truly on display. Two young men with their cocks standing to attention awaited Crystals's next invitation. "Now one of you would surely like to try aunty's other spot?"

Jessica smiled, quite turned on by Crystal's woman-of-great-experience talk. It was obviously working for her so why not keep it going.

The cock in Jessica's cunt suddenly removed itself and she felt a hand touching her.

"Mind if I have another turn? Just in case you don't get to Goulburn or forget me when you do."

Jessica looked up at the radiant face of Brad as his large countryman's hand lifted her red ankle-strapped slutty shoes upward.

"Oh, Brad. Please have a turn. I was just thinking of you and even planning my visit to Bren and Bella's place.

"But what happened to Sasha? Did she change her mind?"

Brad nuzzled the end of his cock in the lips of Jessica's wet vagina and laughed.

"I must have been too good unless she was still really excited by the bloke who was in her before me. She came really quickly so all I could do was spank her arse which made her cum again, and then I left. Would you prefer it fast or slow? I'm happy with either."

Jessica couldn't believe her luck. This man was ticking boxes faster than she could invent them. To have him back and still unspent was a joy.

"I'm happy with either, Brad. But I like having you here so slow might be better and I can ask you difficult questions."

Brad roared laughing and moved his huge cock slowly in to the place where he and Jessica could enjoy themselves.

Jessica had already decided that she was in the early stages of being besotted with Brad and she told herself that whatever she said to him would not really be detrimental to their relationship in any way. So she kicked off with an obvious question.

"Brad! Question number one. Do you have a wife or a permanent girl friend or even someone you really fancy?"

Brad was concentrating on his cock and the delightful pussy it was enjoying.

Jessica let out a groan and then a gasp as Brad's large member made its presence known.

"No to all of those," Brad murmured.

The two enjoyed a quiet moment with their own and each others genitals. Jessica sighed and lifted herself up to meet him then she would back away so that Brad's cock had to follow down her wet tunnel and beg for more. Brad seemed to love that movement.

"Question two, Brad, and don't panic. It's really only a technical question. Other than pregnancy or money, what are the three reasons that you would ask a girl to marry you?"

Brad stopped shagging and Jessica saw him thinking hard, seemingly searching for the right answer. Then he got back on the job and thrust his cock in hard, making her gasp and jerk her body as she felt the beginning of an orgasm.

"Jesus, Jessica! How is a man supposed to answer that. He will know when he finds the right girl. It'll be bloody obvious."

Jessica was now softly panting, knowing that she was heading towards an almighty orgasm. And she wasn't going to let Brad get away with glib answers. Jessica groaned and stretched her body out and tried to close her legs around Brad's neck and fold them there. Now she could see her feet and ankles and her slutty shoes swaying behind Brad's head and her excitement doubled.

"That is not a very good answer, Brad." Jessica whispered between her clenched jaws. "Think about it and try again, as though your life depended on it."

Brad was nearing the moment of truth and so was Jessica, and when they both came, miraculously at the same time, Jessica screamed his name and Brad shouted "Fruit cake."

Brad laid on top of Jessica and stared at her gorgeous face. Brad had seen a lot of gorgeous faces in his short life but this one did things for him that the others hadn't.

Jessica stared back at Brad, incredulous that this man had achieved so much with her emotions so quickly. But she was not confused; far from it.

"Fruit cake? Is that it? I won best fruit cake three years in a row at Armidale Church of England Girls Grammar School, Brad. I'll remember this moment and remember too, that if I'm ever looking for a husband, there is a good chance that my cake making skill will make me a potential winner."

Brad reached forward and put his lips on Jessica's and kissed her gently and lovingly.

"Come to Goulburn and make me a cake, Jessica. And Jessica?"

Suddenly Jessica was doe eyed and emotional.

"Yes Brad?"

"I'm glad we met this way. It's like we cleared two years of potential shit out of a relationship in just a couple of hours.

"I think it wouldn't be hard to be in love with such a beautiful sexy bitch like you, knowing that if we ever needed to, we could both happily go dogging at the old church."

Jessica held Brad tightly to her bosom. She wanted to cry but managed not to.

"Brad?"

"Yes, Jessica?"

"Can people still get married in the dogging church?"

Brad nestled his enormous but softening cock in Jessica's pussy and sighed.

"Well, I reckon it is possible. My family own it after all."

———

The young men had all left, all seemingly with a healthy look of satisfaction. The three women were in the tea room having a cup of tea and a chocolate biscuit. They were understandable subdued even though they were very happy.

Sasha spoke about her night first.

"I think this was my best night ever. The lads all rallied around and did the right thing by me. There wasn't a slack cock amongst them and I believe they all had a great time. What about you, Crystal?"

Crystal reached for a second biscuit.

"My night was good too. I couldn't believe how well my playing the cruise ship who wants to be fucked by all the deck-hands, played with the boys imagination. They all responded really well. And now I'm sure there will be a few who might consider going to sea."

Jessica yelled out her support for Crystal.

"I managed to perv on Crystal a couple of times and I was quite envious. She really had the right words flowing to keep the boys giving her all they could. I'm hoping I can come up with something similar for my next time. Maybe telling them how innocent and inexperienced I was and asking them to help me. That might get them going?"

Sasha looked closely at Jessica.

"I think you did very well, Jess. From what I saw, you had your hands full along with everything else. You even stole one of my favourites.

"Brad Braithwaite seemed a little less than enthusiastic when he got to me after being with you.

"I know him quite well as does Crystal who comes from near where his family live. We had arranged a fantasy about him being my bad boy cousin but he couldn't do the deed.

"I don't know what happened between you two but I sense he has a soft spot for you. I saw him shortly afterwards giving it to you like he meant it. Best of luck with that, you cousin stealing slut."

They all laughed but Jessica was thinking about what Sasha had said. Was it possible that she was right. Did Brad really have a thing for her? Jessica's heart was pounding as she thought about Brad and how when she held him tight, she felt something she's never felt with a man before. Then she smiled, thinking about him and presenting him with a fruit cake.

"What does Brad do? I know that his parents have a farm property. I guess he works on the farm? If so, what is he doing in Sydney?"

Sasha eyed Jessica with amusement.

"Ah ha! Me thinks that maybe the lady is interested?"

Jessica felt herself blushing.

"Brad has been in Sydney for a month studying something to do with his course. He is in his final year at Charles Sturt Veterinary school at Wagga but occasionally he attends short courses at the Sydney University of Technology. That is how I met him along with some of his mates.

"He's a great bloke and he will make a great vet. I'd let him fix up my pussy anytime. And a woman I spoke to recently commented that in her experience, vets who work with large farm animals are really great at fisting. Go figure, girls."

Much laughter ensued as the three satisfied ladies collected their bits and pieces and headed off. Sasha called out as they stepped out into the warm night air.

"Are you sexy sluts interested in another night if I get one organised?"

Crystal answered first. "Only if they are old enough to respond to my experienced older woman fantasies. As someone once said, when you find something that works for you, stay with it."

Jessica said her goodbye's, adding that she would happily present herself for a repeat of this evenings entertainment.

When Jessica had showered and slipped into her nightie, she wandered over to the bookshelf. There it was. Grandma's original copy of the Country Womens Association Cookbook.

Fruit cakes were suddenly what Jessica wanted to think about and she smiled to herself.

"I wonder if Brad likes peel or not? You can never be sure with fruit cake. Some people love peel and others don't. Now how can I find out?"

Jessica recalled watching a friend of Prue when they were at school together. Ingrid had sat with them at the table in the common room, picking out every piece of citrus peel in a slice of Jessica's latest fruit cake masterpiece.

Jessica knew that she wanted to get to know Brad better and she knew he liked fruit cake. The more she thought about it the more she was convinced that this man would eat cake with peel or without it. She would make her usual cake and that was that. Then she suddenly recalled something she had read in a magazine. *Men are all alike - except the one you've met who's different*

Lookout Brad!

18

BEST JOB IN THE WORLD

JESSICA WAS OFFERED employment to work at a function organised by a friend of Robyn's. This was pitched as a house party but only for grown ups. Its real purpose was not in doubt; men and women getting together. Swinging by a different name.

This was the third of Robyn's close friend Ursula's monthly get togethers and with word of what was offered spreading fast, it was now drawing in people from other genteel suburbs close by.

Jessica came to the house early as suggested, and introduce herself to Ursula who welcomed her with the full up and down visual inspection. Ursula smiled her approval with what she saw. Jessica immediately saw that Ursula fitted the same mould as Robyn; a voluptuous older woman with what Jessica suspected was a suspiciously similar sexual appetite.

As instructed, Jessica had dressed conservatively, wearing black slacks, a white polar-necked skivvy and low heeled black shoes. Her hair was tied up in a bun. She had been told on the phone that in no way was she to compete with the party-goers. If Jess had dressed in the clothes that she usually wore when she strutted her stuff at parties, then she would have been seen as obvious competition to the female guests and indeed, a major distraction.

"Robyn said you were intelligent and looked good and suggested you would be the right person to be my eyes and ears and general help. From what I'm seeing, it looks as though she was right.

"I'm sure you will understand, darling, when I say that you should not tempt our visitors from either the partner they arrive with or the person they are hoping to connect with. Not that you aren't allowed to enjoy yourself. Just maybe fill your own needs later in the evening with a little something on the side although nothing that would attract too much attention."

"I have quite a lot of experience, Ursula and I can assure you that my desires are well controlled," Jessica replied with a reassuring smile.

"Now I've made this pin for you Jessica. I suggest you wear it to officially inform people of your status and also to help avoid unwanted advances."

Ursula leant forward and gently pinned the label on Jessica's chest. It read: Jessica: Information and Party Advice.

Jessica bathed Ursula in her most disarming smile.

Ursula smiled back.

"Make yourself known to the head waitress. Her name is Inala and I've told her about you. I hope you enjoy yourself. If your presence tonight works for both of us, Jessica, then I will be looking to employ you on a regular basis.

"Oh yes! There is one more thing you should know. I've implemented a second feature to the evenings entertainment which not many people will discover but which I think will become popular over time. I call it The Dunking Paddock and it's basically a private dogging venue situated out in the little paddock which can be reached via a gate in the back wall at the far end of the garden.

"It is free to members but will also be available as a stand alone event sometime soon. Men attending on their own will pay to enter. Women will be admitted free but for safety's sake they need to be accompanied by a male partner; a husband, brother or whatever.

"Not sure yet how it will go. You could keep an eye out and let me know what you think. Ultimately it will be up to the ladies whether or not it will work. If they like it then we'll keep it going."

Ursula smiled and suggested Jessica wander about and familiarise herself with the house.

"The lights are dimmed throughout the house. There are many rooms and nooks and cranny's which you will discover.

"One last thing that I should mention. There is one very large room on the ground floor where I've taken out the walls between three bedrooms. We call this The Pink room because it is lit with a subdued pink lighting. The floor is covered in mattresses, pillows and cushions and it is the place where most find their way to eventually and where they can offer themselves to all. An open market, so to speak.

"I've given you a tiny bedroom at the top of the stairs where you can put your bag and coat or just get a moment to yourself. Here is the key. First door on the left. Oh yes. I've put a small pocket torch on the bed which you may wish to carry for emergency use. Have fun darling. I'll hopefully be very busy so any questions you have should be made to Inala and not to me."

Jessica thanked Ursula and picked up her bag and headed up the wide staircase. She deposited her things on the bed in her room and thought what a great little hideaway it was. The little torch seemed like a good idea so she popped into her pocket.

Just as she was about to leave, Jessica remembered something and went back to her bag. She had bought herself a present on-line. Jessica smiled and gently fondled it. She decided to wear it tonight, just to get used to the feel of having it there. A little lubricant helped and suddenly she was in charge of the new toy and thinking how big it felt but then she assumed she would soon adjust to it.

A pink ribbon belt fell out of the box and Jessica stared at it, wondering what it was for. Then she looked at the instruction leaflet and smiled then wrapped the ribbon around herself and tightened it. Now she could see why it was a good idea. It held everything tight against her belly and made the new thingy practically invisible inside her panties and slacks.

Wandering about the house looking in all of the rooms and noticing the hidden alcoves was exciting. A narrow back stairway lead to what must have once been servants quarters. Doors led to tiny rooms each housing a single bed with hardly room to move.

In the fading light, she inspected the garden and even ventured into The Dunking Paddock which boasted a number of solid double bed-like wooden bases spread about, each topped with a soft straw-filled palliasse.

When she felt she had a reasonable mental picture of the property in her head, Jessica went back to where she could observe the large room and main reception area, peering between the steps of the wide open staircase. Then she ventured out and found a deep arm chair to bury herself in, just near where the stairs began and alongside the entrance to the ground floor passageway.

Observing people arriving and reading their body language was most enjoyable, as was assessing people by their looks. Jessica looked forward to listening in to their conversations where possible. The whole idea excited her. This was her night to be the absolute voyeur.

A few people had already been shown through to the big lounge room.

One couple had seated themselves on one of the three large settees and were holding hands and looking both at each other and towards the door, watching to see others arriving.

Then a party of three arrived. Jessica figured that the two largish women were probably sisters in their mid forties and the man would have been a husband of one of them or perhaps an older brother or maybe just a friend.

Big smiles on big ladies and eager looks of anticipation radiated around the room as the group moved to take a seat on a settee. After they had sunk into the soft cushions, both women instinctively moved their hands to pull down the hems of their short skirts over their chubby legs to try to give a sense of modesty, not that it made a lot of difference. Their heavy stockinged legs and tight strappy high heels along with their exaggerated make-up signalled they were dressed for an evening of fun or maybe debauchery.

Jessica realised that she was already loving this job. Watching people prepare for a night of sexual adventure was truly exciting.

The first couple she had noticed suddenly decided to move and rose and headed towards the settee close to Jessica but as they were about to sit down, the man turned and looked towards the door and Jessica heard him speak.

"They're here darling. Look! I said they'd come."

His partner stopped staring across at Jessica and looked back to the main door.

"Oh yes, Arnold, they did come. I'm so pleased to see them. I just hope they remember us and are pleased to see us."

Arnold waved across the room and Jessica saw a man and woman waving back and moving slowly across to join the first couple.

"Well Megan. Happy now? I know how much you enjoyed Ray."

The lovely lady's face took on the perfect blush and she looked at Arnold with a kindly knowing smile. Then, without any indication to her man, she looked quickly past him across at the nearby Jessica and beamed a beautiful smile.

"And I believe you enjoyed his lovely wife just as much, darling. I just hope they remember us as fondly. From my memory, Susannah was blown away when you took her up against the wall."

Arnold laughed.

"As I remember it, you both came at about the same time. Ray nailed you against the same wall and it all took off from there."

Jessica was wildly excited by what she was hearing. On top of that, she was instantly in love with the lithe wifey Megan, staring at her in her floral dress and seamed stockings and modest heels. Jessica suddenly found herself wanting to lie on top of Megan and do loving things with her beautiful and seemingly innocent body.

"Maybe those American TV shows depicting attractive bored housewives were really true to life after all?" Jessica mused.

As the newly arrived couple came closer, Jessica noticed certain similarities. Both women were tall and lithe and both stood a half head higher than their husbands. The men were stocky and likely quite muscular.

"Hi, Arnold and Megan. So glad you are here. Susannah was terrified you wouldn't show up. I assured her that you seemed to have as good a time as us when we first met so you were sure to be here."

Jessica was now in love with all four. Susannah in a plain summer frock and stockings and heels was almost identical to the lovely Megan. And Jess could have willingly allowed either or both of the two jolly men to pin her against a wall and do what ever they wanted.

There was an awkward moment of silence as the two couples continued smiling at each other, neither pair sure of what to say or do next. Jessica noticed the excitement shining through the blushes on both womens faces and she tried to live their anticipation.

Then Susannah reached across and took Megan's hand and Jessica saw Megan squeeze the other's hand signifying a common purpose. Then in a little voice, Megan spoke.

"We both liked what we did last time and would happily do it again if that is okay with you boys? And, I should ask, if you are both still okay with us gals getting it from other men later? And we so loved seeing you with other women didn't we Susannah?"

Susanna grinned. "Oh, yes. Especially towards the end when that very big lady made you both fuck her, and then suggested you both try to fuck her at the same time. Megan and I were both quietly cheering you on. It was so hot."

Arnold and Raymond exchanged glances, silently indicating that a repeat of last time was exactly what they wanted. Then each took the hand of their partner and placed it in the hand of the other man.

Jessica saw the smiles widen on the faces of the two ladies as they saw that it was all about to happen and she knew exactly what they were feeling. In fact, at that moment Jessica felt the exact same excitement and noticed that the crotch of her knickers were suddenly feeling moist despite the presence of her new toy.

As the two happy couples turned towards the staircase, it was all Jessica could do to not get up and follow them.

"Oh my god! This job might be too exciting. I will need to be a little more careful about how close I get to peoples fantasies."

Jessica looked back to where the couples were just disappearing at the top of the stair and she thought how, in only a few moments, Arnold and Raymond will have the pants off Susannah and Megan and be happily climbing under those summer frocks and in between the girls beautiful thighs and shafting the two of them against a lucky upstairs wall. Bliss!

It was good that the four lovers had gone. Now Jessica could get back to work and concentrate on what was happening in the large lounge. The big ladies had disappeared although the male member of the group was still near the sofa in conversation with two men.

Jessica scolded herself for not being more observant and chastised herself severely. Then she saw the big ladies emerge from the door that led to the bathroom and walk over to the settee. Two men had arrived and were talking with the womens companion and each turned and held out a hand, then they led the women away along the corridor beside the stairs, heading no doubt, to one of the many bedrooms.

Things were definitely getting busier and Jessica realised that she wouldn't be able to scrutinise all of the people to the same degree that she had so far.

Couples wandered everywhere. Quite a number were women in pairs but most comprised a man and one or sometimes, two woman.

Jessica saw a group of three men in their late thirties or early forties, checking out the women spread around the lounge. They seemed to be targeting women on their own or women in pairs or at least those without a male partner. The men would approach a woman and after a few moments Jessica would see a woman nodding her head indicating a negative response and the men would move away. They were seemingly being knocked back by every woman they approached and Jessica tried to guess what the men were proposing.

As Jessica scanned the crowd, she noticed that the three men were heading towards a tiny woman who had caught Jessica's attention earlier. It wasn't just her diminutive size that was interesting. The woman was dressed in a most sexually provocative manner, much more sexually overt than anyone else in the room. She wore a low cut red top and a very short and tight red miniskirt. Her slender legs were sheathed in white stay-up stockings topped with frills and her strappy red sandals could not have had higher heels.

There was something else about this little lady. She seemed very active, or was she agitated? She stood up and sat down constantly and fiddled with the hem of her short mini skirt and sometimes lifted a leg and removed a high stiletto shoe and inspected it and then immediately refitted it to her tiny foot.

Jessica wondered if the woman was okay. Maybe she was exhibiting signs of the affects of an illicit substance? Jessica couldn't be sure.

Just as Jessica thought she should wander over and see if help was needed, the three men approached and began a conversation with the tiny sexy looking woman. It was only moments before Jessica saw the woman nodding in agreement. Then she took hold of two of the mens hands and let them lead her down the passage beside the stairs.

Jessica knew enough to guess what was being offered by the men and she wondered if the little lady had any inkling of what she was in for. If she didn't then her first gang bang was likely to be a shock but Jessica reasoned that maybe this was what the woman was desperately wanting; and who was Jessica to assume otherwise or pass judgement. At least there was a modicum of care in selecting who was admitted to this event and hopefully there would be a level of civility among the three men so that their sexual encounter would be satisfying to all parties. Jessica prayed that this would be so.

Things were moving faster. Not only that, a number of the increasingly large throng now overflowing the lounge were showing early signs of losing their inhibitions as a result of simply drinking a glass or two of Champagne or simply being carried along with the euphoria of anticipation. This was manifesting itself in a sudden increase in touching and feeling of bodies by both sexes.

Respectable looking women had hands pressed up against the bulging fronts of mens trousers even as they remained holding hands with the man they had arrived with. One woman had already unzipped her suitor and was gently massaging his potent looking hard-on.

More often than not, the man whose crotch a woman had her hand on, had a hand not just on the woman's backsides but even under her skirt or dress, inadvertently displaying an elegant silk clad leg or even the woman's skimpy-panty clad backside and which she might wriggle provocatively in anticipation.

Jessica watched as two such women smiled as each handed their partner over to the other. Then the newly connected couples smiled and then one lead the way towards the stairway, followed by the other two, hands gently groping each other as they went.

Across the room, more people were arriving.

Of interest was the older Japanese man accompanied by three younger women. Two of the women could easily have been sisters and looked to be of Caribbean extraction. They looked extraordinarily beautiful from where Jessica was sitting.

The third woman looked to be part Japanese and was also stunningly attractive in a different sort of way. She was petite and her cropped spiked orange and green hair made her the centre of attention, in particular the attention of many of the women in the room.

More people were partnering and setting off to discover secluded spots in the house where they could give vent to their lust.

Twice, Jessica watched as an older woman was led away by two younger men. She also noticed a well built swarthy man with a shiny bald head being led away by two women who acted both nervous and excited. They kissed every few moments, maybe to reassure each other on their choice of action. Each took turns in grasping the sizeable bulge in the man's trousers even while their faces showed red with embarrassment. Tales of the potency of bald men were obviously alive and well.

Jessica couldn't resist exploring her voyeur instincts more thoroughly and decided to follow the crowd even though she was the only one without a partner. She began by taking a stroll along the dimly lit passageway and discovered that what some folk were doing could be both funny or erotic or both.

"Is that you Henry? I've left my glasses in my bag and you know I'm lost without them when I'm in a dark space. It doesn't feel like you but whoever it is, it does feel nice. If you're not Henry, perhaps you should tell me your name if you are intending to get intimate with me. Even if I cannot see you properly at least I'll know who I was with. And while I'm thinking about it, where are we going?"

There was silence, then a woman's voice close by answered.

"I think you've got my George, Lottie, and I'm pretty sure that what I've got in my hand belongs to your Henry. Is it okay if he knobs me darling? George will give you a good go, I'm sure. A couple of drinks and he usually wants it doggy style. And he'll go forever. Just thought you should know. I'm sure you will love it."

There was silence for a moment as Charlotte reviewed her situation.

"Well, Harriet. If we both enjoy being knobbed by each others, I suppose it could be something we can do at home. Would you be up for it? Sending them over on a Sunday afternoon could become something we did instead of going for a drive."

"Indeed! Being knobbed sounds much better than going to a plant nursery or art gallery. And if it works, we could ask our neighbours Doreen and Stacey if they were interested in doing it. I reckon both of their blokes could be good for something a little different.

Jessica couldn't stop herself giggling and thought how this must be the best paid job in the whole world. Then she heard voices coming from a bedroom and stopped and peeped inside.

"For goodness sake, if you're brothers then surely you must know who usually goes first?"

A well built attractive older woman had stripped down to just her stockings and shoes and was sitting back on the bed with her legs wide apart and her hairy vagina on full display. Her large solid breasts stood out provocatively and she held a solid cock in each hand.

Jessica had noticed the woman earlier and watched as the hands of the two young men were offered by another older woman. The mens mother perhaps? After the three headed off down the passageway the woman who handed them over stared after them then took out a handkerchief and dabbed her eyes.

"No, please stop it? We're not going to do the eeny-meeny miny-moe thing again. I've caught my tigers by their cocks so just give it me. However much you holler, I'm not letting either of you go. One of you just fuck me. Now! Or is there something else going on?

"Okay! Just in case I've missed something, feel free to call me mummy if that helps. Now! Mummy would like a cuddle please."

There was a sudden a flurry of activity and the lady on the bed was suddenly rolled onto her knees with her bum in the air and vocalising her excitement. Between screams she managed to whisper. "Christ! So that's how she did it?"

Jessica closed the door quietly, still giggling and set out along the passageway. Surely someone somewhere must be just lustfully doing it, she thought.

When Jessica neared the bend in the passageway she at last heard the plaintive tones of a "Yes! Yes! Yes! Harder you beautiful bastard," and she thought the world was at last working the way it should. She gently pushed open a door and peered into the gloom.

The two big ladies she had watched leave with two men earlier were on their knees on a big bed, heaving their bodies every which way. Their huge buttocks were slapping in noisey unison as the two strong males shoved energetically into their pussies.

"Have you bitches had enough yet?" said one of the men, quietly.

"Or are your wet cunts ready for another round?" echoed the other man.

Jessica heard the women sobbing and wailing and wondered if they were okay. Then a cracked voice called out.

"Give us some more cock. Just get on with it."

The two men pulled out and swapped places then reinserted themselves in the wet hairy places being so generously offered.

"Okay Spike. Lets go!"

The women screamed and began thrusting their rear ends back up to meet their pleasure providers.

"Yes! Yes! Yes!"

Again, Jessica backed out of the room quietly.

Time had moved on. People all over the house were doing it as Jessica wandered happily along the passage until she came to the door marked The Pink Room. She could hear a low hum of voices and sounds. At first she thought it better that she not go in in case she was seen as another person of interest. But then she thought again and decided that she probably needed to see what was going on simply to get on-the-job experience about something she had not yet seen.

Jessica went in and found a spot to hide beside the coat and dress racks behind the door.

Jess saw that this is were it all really happens late in the day. The grand finale; if a girl hadn't had enough elsewhere, here is where she should end the evening.

There were at least forty bodies spread across the room and across each other. Legs and backsides waved in the air and there was an enormous amount of thrusting going on.

Jessica noticed that there were many woman embracing and kissing and touching each other. Whether they were on their hands and knees being fucked doggy style or on their backs getting a standard shafting, at least half the ladies had a hand exploring the woman laying next to her. It was then that Jessica spotted Megan and Susannah. Both were on their knees each getting a slow doggy shagging by keen and determined males. On either side of them, women who were also receiving an energetic workout from a man, reached out to fondle the breasts of Jessica's two favourite housewives.

Jessica looked around the floor in search of Arnold and Raymond and eventually she discovered them at opposite ends of the room, each with a woman sitting on them, energetically rising up and down on their cocks and seemingly mouthing words or sounds that Jessica could not decipher above the noise.

Both men seemed happy with their situations and they were obviously happy in the knowledge that their wives on the other side of the room were getting well and truly poked.

Jessica was about to leave when she recognised a voice. A woman close by was humping another woman.

The women underneath her was gasping and writhing under the energetic attention she was enjoying.

"How come you haven't done this to me before, Hetty?"

"Never thought about it until I saw those two women over there doing it. I'm loving it Charlotte. I hope you are. Give me your hand. I want it between my legs."

Jessica looked around and noted that indeed, there were a number of women atop other women. In some instances they were part of a threesome being recipients of male attention from the rear.

"I'm loving it Harriet. Maybe we could do this at each others after morning tea on a Wednesday when the boys are at golf?"

"I think I'm going to want it more often than that, Lottie so look out. We've got a lot of catching up to do."

As Harriet rubbed herself vigorously on Charlotte's large pubic mound, she felt a hand on her back. Looking up and to the side, she observed a beautiful woman smiling at her. Then the woman spoke, quietly mouthing her words "That is so beautiful. I'd love to be your friend. I'm Megan."

Harriet slowed down and stared at Megan.

"Why not! I'm Harriet Jones. I'm the only one listed. Call me, Megan. I'd love that."

Jessica headed back along the shadowy corridor to return to her watching station. Women on their knees on the carpet were sucking a host of cocks as well as breasts and pussies while others leant against the walls of the passage with their legs apart and their knees bent. Men yelled and women screamed.

Happiness reigned and out in the lounge room, a couple of women who had been enjoying themselves in the Pink Room and now thought they were finished for the day, were now smiling contentedly. But suddenly they were astonished to find themselves the centre of attention. Now they were being bent over the backs of armchairs, and their dresses dragged up over their backsides by men who had happily discovered that they still had shots in their armoury and could offer a final ravishing. On seeing what was happening, other men were suddenly discovering that they too had something left and began to line up for a turn.

Only moments after she returned to stand close by her comfy chair, now home to a trouser-less man and two disheveled ladies, Jessica's world changed dramatically.

Suddenly an arm encircled Jessica's waist then a small hand slid up under her skivvy and her little bra, grasping her girly breast while another arm put her neck in a stranglehold.

"I know what you need lovely lady and I'm the only person who can give it to you. Is it to be here on the carpet or do you have a preferred place? Answer me quickly you skinny bitch."

Jessica smelt a rare perfume and the elegant voice of a woman was mesmerising. She was immediately in love with her assailant.

"The alcove just behind the stairs," Jessica gurgled despite the choking hold around her throat.

In just moments Jessica was on her back in a darkened spot which the passing crowed seemed never to notice. Hands were removing her clothing and suddenly she was in just her little red bra and matching hold ups.

"I knew it. I can spot one from across the room. But you won't have this for long darling or at least not until I've finished with you.

Jessica's new strapless dildo stood up, waving its head, happy to be released from her knickers and the pink restraining strap.

Above her loomed the beautiful lesbian with the orange and green spiked hair and Jessica could see that the woman was wearing a rubber cock like her own and she knew that she was about to be fucked with it.

Jessica's body screamed with excitement. This is what she really really wanted. Life had been leading her towards this moment. A full lesbian showdown – woman to woman and no men allowed.

"What will I call you?" Jessica gasped.

"Sara! And you?"

"Jessica!"

Sara fondled Jessica between the legs and gently removed her strapless toy. Then without further talk or action, Sara inserted her rubber cock into Jessica and began a rigorous dance of love that Jessica would never forget.

"Oh Sara. Yes! Yes!"

Jessica looked up into the eyes of her new magic mistress and smiled with glazed eyes, heaving herself upward every once in a while as Sara moved backward and forward to a different tune. Sara's eyes were often closed and her small smiling mouth would pout and sometimes she would moan in her obvious ecstasy.

Jessica didn't know how long the two woman had been standing watching her and Sara make love, but when she heard one of them speak she thought she'd gone to heaven.

"Now that is what a girl really needs, Susannah."

Megan and her friend were enthralled and both women watched with their hands up under their skirts.

Jessica moved her head and looked up at the two gorgeous women, then before she could stop herself, she smiled her most loving smile and patted the carpet on either side of her and her lover, gesturing to them to lie down beside them, and without a moments hesitation, the two slid down and laid back on the carpet and stared closely at the beautiful lovemaking scene before them.

When Sara became aware that she had an audience, she stopped what she was doing and looked at each of them. Then, in that beautiful Kentish private school voice she spoke.

"Please make yourselves comfortable ladies and don't go away. My name is Sara. You will be next; and you can touch us if you wish."

Then she buried the rubber cock deep in Jessica's cunt and Jessica screamed and orgasmed.

Sara removed herself and gently returned Jessica's dildo to her, placing it back in what was now a well lubricated vagina. Then she moved over and lowered herself between the legs of a stupefied Susannah who squealed and spoke gibberish as she excitedly reached forward with both hands to take hold of Sara's rubber gift and pull it towards her crotch.

"Now, you straight slutty house wife. You will never forget the moment when I made you see that you should give yourself to a women. I'm going to make you appreciate true pussy power. You want that don't you, you sexy little tart? Cunts as well as cocks will be your future and you will thank me for that."

Sara pushed into the more than ready randy woman beneath her and Susannah let out a piercing scream and began to gasp loudly and call out.

"Yes! Oh yes, Sara. Show me the way; I want it! I want it!"

Then Sara leant forward and engulfed Susannah's mouth and sucked out her tongue.

Now it was Jessica's and Megan's turn.

"I fell in love with you the moment I saw you sitting in the arm chair, Jessica."

Megan put out her hand and touched Jessica's face and then leant forward and kissed her on the lips and moments later they were fully immersed in a kissing frenzy.

"I wanted you too. You are so beautiful. I want you so much and I will keep wanting you."

The two women hugged each other, kissing and sighing as they did so.

"You can shag me with that thing if you want to, Jessica," Megan whispered. "Whatever you want my darling. I just want you every which way, and very likely I will want you in my life forever."

Jessica gently slid herself on top of Megan and their hands felt each other in excited anticipation and they both sighed and groaned with the intense feelings they were experiencing.

With their lips pressed hard together, Jessica parted Megan's legs and rested the end of her rubber cock against her neat lightly haired and extremely wet vagina.

"Oh Megan! I give you this with my love."

Jessica gently pushed into Megan whose vagina seemed to just open and swallow her rubber offering and suddenly their bodies were gently moving together in a dance of passion.

"Oh my God! Oh yes! Please Jessica. I love you! I will want much more of this."

There came a moment when all four women paused and reviewed their situations. Then Sara spoke.

"The only way a woman can free herself from the restrictive male dominated ethos is to enjoy making love to women as well as to men.

"Now go forth and seduce your friends and neighbours, young and old. Let female love lead the way and free you from disappointment. You will never regret it."

Sara dressed and put her clothes in order, hiding her male appendage beneath her elasticised knickers. She smiled at everyone and murmured a "thank you" then headed off across the room towards her companions.

Susannah rolled over and smiled at Megan and Jessica.

"Can I have a little bit of your friend, Megan? Right now I just want to be fucked by a woman for ever. Pretty please? And we must get ourselves a couple of these rubber doodads. We are definitely going to need them from now on."

Megan smiled down at Jessica and took hold of her rubber cock and rubbed it.

"Could you give my friend a little a bit of this my love? I can see that like me, she is going to want a lot of it in the future."

Jessica smiled up at her new love. Then she rolled over and pushed Susannah back down on the carpet and slowly shagged the woman who groaned and called out while Megan lightly fingered Jessica's buttocks and breasts and kissed her shoulders and her neck and her back and whispered, "Yes! Yes! Fuck the lovely bitch, my darling. Then give it to me again. I love you."

But Jessica was forced to stop and she looked at the two women and said how she should be getting back to work or she might get the

BEST JOB IN THE WORLD | 161

sack. They all laughed and kissed and Megan gave Jessica her telephone number and made her promise to call.

––––––––––

Back at her watching station beside the arm chair, Jessica saw that everyone had indeed moved on. Disheveled people who had obviously finished their escapades were appearing from the passageway and others staggered down the stairs. They milled around the room looking at each other seemingly in no hurry to leave.

A couple of women seemed to have mislaid their dresses, adorning the room in just their underwear and shoes, casually signalling their satisfaction with the happy sensual experiences they had recently enjoyed. Many wore dreamy smiles while others looked dazed, even shocked.

Most seemed oblivious to her, but then Jessica felt a hand on her backside. The tiny woman who had gone off with the three men was standing and looking at Jessica. She beamed up at her, reading her name tag, and in a tiny low voice, announced that her name was Milly and she needed a woman to finish her off and she had worked out that Jessica would be the best person to help her.

Looking at the tiny sexy apparition beside her and trying to focus on the woman's request was at first a shock. But then, still hot from her most recent adventure, Jessica smiled and mumbled "Sure! Love to! Follow me, Milly." and taking the woman by the hand, led her up the stairs to her room.

The tiny Milly melted under Jessica's wanton lesbian advances, taking delight in screaming and thrusting her lovely body every which way. Jessica was giving Milly exactly what she wanted and what Jessica wanted too. Milly gurgled and moaned and called out for more and her legs pointed to the ceiling and waved as Jessica worked her magic with the rubber dildo. But that wasn't all. Jessica was so excited by Milly that she wanted to eat her and biting the woman and yelling at her that she was a gang-banging slut, fuelled both womens deepest desires.

"Oh yes, Jessica. I'm a gang-banging slut. Punish me you darling woman."

When Milly came, Jessica feared she had done the doll-like creature an injury. A plaintive wail issued from Milly's lips and she shook constantly for what seemed like forever, then she was still. Jessica stared down at a seemingly lifeless body.

Then Milly's eyes opened and she smiled a beautiful smile and reached up to pull Jessica's head down to be kissed.

"Save the best till last, I always say. Can I give you my telephone number Jessica? You know how to give a girl what she really needs"

Jessica laughed and rolled off.

"I must get back to work, Milly. And yes. Give me your number and I will give you mine. We will fuck again. You are a delight."

Jessica saw that the crowd had thinned and it seemed that people were leaving in a very happy state of mind. Then she remembered being asked to check on the activities in the little paddock out the back. The Dunking area as Ursula referred to it and she quickly made her way out the back and through the garden area.

As she approached the paddock she could hear sounds through the gate so she knew that something was happening.

Jessica had experienced real dogging. Jessica had twice been privileged to be a part of a select dogging group, once in Sydney and also a similar event in the disused churchyard near Goulburn. Both were classic dogging situations involving vehicles, but with the benefit of exclusive membership. No smelly pervy types allowed.

The Dunking was different. There were no vehicles' from where a women could take shelter or tease the many men lining up at the car window, exposing themselves and looking forward to the woman in the car lowering the window so that she could take a lucky cock in her hand. Or if the men were really lucky, she might open the door and offer herself, and from there, she might be led or carried out onto the grass to be properly ravished.

Jessica found herself reminiscing and increased her pace to more quickly discover what was happening behind the wall.

Participation at The Dunking was greater than Jessica expected it would be. Most of the beds were in use plus some people were laying directly on the grass or on blankets.

The two big ladies had moved in, sharing a mattress and sharing the line-up of stiff cocks. They no longer had any clothes on except shoes and they were excitedly flaunting their enormous and insatiable rear ends to the line-up of cock-wagging males awaiting their turn. And Jessica could just make out that it wasn't the usual love hole that was being filled.

Jessica could have stopped and stood and watched the anal attacks but there was so much more to look at.

Wherever Jessica looked, a line of men stood waiting their turn to place their cock in a woman. In some cases they stood in a circle around a woman who selected them randomly to suck. It was then that she realised that this wasn't dogging as she knew it but rather a huge gang-bang. Fun it might well be, but it lacked the excitement potential of proper dogging.

Women need to be in control and also enjoy the anticipation of not knowing what might happen next. The Dunking was all too blatantly predictable. It might work for someone once, but less so the next time.

Wandering quietly among the participants, trying not to attract male attention, Jessica could see that for a number of women, this was a totally new experience and they seemed to be enjoying the novelty of it.

Her eyes were drawn to two women who were kneeling on a blanket with a row of men standing in line behind them.

As she drew closer, she realised that she had seen the women earlier and had overheard parts of their conversation.

It appears that they were next-door neighbours and both recently divorced and totally loving their new found freedom. That freedom had also involved them becoming lovers so that when Jessica first saw them, they were holding hands and enthusiastically talking to two other women who were also holding hands.

"Oh we like to have men too, but since we became single and got together, life has changed. We are never lonely. And if we need a cock, we just drag in one of our neighbours who are always willing to give it to us. Their wives know about us and their husbands, and they are happy for all of us. And it gives them time to themselves to do what they want to do, be it to make love to someone elses husband or their girlfriends. Win, win all around, we think."

Jessica mused that what the two were getting now would no doubt serve them well for quite some time. She also couldn't help thinking that they would need a good 'finishing off' later; but then they had each other for that.

It was late in the evening when Jessica's boss appeared. Ursula looked immaculate and without any sign that she had been a party to an adventure of any sort.

"Hello Jess. I managed to take a shower and change. Always worth freshening up after a busy night.

"How has it been, darling? Everyone seemed happy as they left and all reports point to a successful outcome for all. Is that how you see it Jessica? Would you say that everyone left with a happy look on their faces?"

Jessica smiled back, watching Ursula relax and unfurl as she ended her day.

"From what I observed, everyone went with a happy-ever-after look on their face. Couldn't have been better, really. And I thoroughly enjoyed myself, Ursula."

Ursula looked long and hard at Jessica.

"And were you able to fit in a moment of pleasure for yourself, darling?"

Jessica found herself unexpectedly colouring up.

"Yes I did, Ursula. All in the line of duty really, I suppose you'd say. Pleasant surprises often. And I really enjoyed watching and listening to people. The voyeur in me was totally stimulated and satisfied."

Ursula laughed and continued to stare at Jessica.

"Was there a high point that a girl might mention?"

Jessica coloured up again.

"It wouldn't be proper to talk about the clients, surely? But I fell in love at least twice and then one amazing lady with spiky green and orange hair had her way with me before I could do a thing to stop her."

Ursula leant back and laughed out loud.

"That was Sara. I sent her to you. Thought you would enjoy something a little different; and from an expert, too. The four in her party are visiting from England and all are exceptionally talented people."

Jessica stared back at her boss.

"Well that is good to know. Having such a caring sharing boss is very rare. Thank you Ursula."

Ursula reached out and took Jessica's hand and drew her close, and fixed her with her beautiful smile.

"Let me kiss you Jess. Maybe one day we will have time to play girly games together. Would you like that?"

Jessica leant towards her boss and puckered up to enjoy the warmth of those large lipsticked lips and in a little voice whispered, "I would like that very much, Ursula."

End

CATCH UP

EROS CRESCENT

No one on Eros Crescent remembers exactly the moment when the words COVID-19 or Corona virus were first uttered in their houses. Needless to say, it would first have been heard on a television report and the importance of the message would have taken a few days to sink in.

The world suddenly changed. Words and phrases like lockdown and self-isolation and social distancing were suddenly in the forefront of all conversations as people enacted the requests of government and the nation to act responsibly to assist in the national objective to achieve what quickly became known as flattening the curve.

For Roger, life couldn't have been less affected. His daily routines required only that he rose from his bed, showered and shaved, ate his breakfast, went for a walk, and made sure he had sufficient pens and paper. Although it did impinge on his new paying project.

He had been asked by Desley to write another booklet similar to the one he'd written for The Club, only this was to be for The Dunking, a venue he had not yet visited or, until now, even heard of.

When Desley explained the concept and related what the setting inside the warehouse was like, Roger was very keen to get started. But the arrival of the virus put an end to that project, at least until further notice.

———

For Caroline and Jackie and Miranda, staying at home was what they enjoyed anyway, that is when they weren't travelling abroad or window shopping or having coffee in cafe's.

All three women had worked in executive positions in London, but moving overseas brought that era to a close, although they had been invited to join similar companies in Australia.

A top of the range coffee making machine was promptly ordered along with a supply of fair trade East Timorese Maubisse, medium blend. Browsing online shops became the new window shopping.

Instagram took on a new importance as the pandemic took hold around the world. Stories and pictures of people in isolation doing amazing and sometime ridiculous things became the rage. Jackie uploaded hundreds of images of the inside and outside of the house, earning the praise of interior designers and architects.

———

Helen and her husband Frederico were effected in so far as Freddy's job as a flight controller at the airport was soon to be reduced in the number of hours he worked. However, there was no threat to his income as he was on standby as an essential service. But Helen's work as a freelance Human Resources consultant to industry came to a sudden halt. She embraced online conferencing on Zoom but this was no substitute for real hands-on consulting.

Helen was also restricted in her love life, already reduced as a result of her husbands responsibilities to Helen's two lovers who had inadvertently become pregnant to him.

Sophie and Freya now spent a night a fortnight with Freddy. Unable to visit or have visits from her own lovers, Polly or Celia Ashbee, Helen would just have to manage with her next-door neighbour, Mary. And what looked like the answer to maiden's prayer, The Club had been forced to close.

Mary's only loss of employment was her volunteer job at the Salvation Army Opportunity Shop which she would miss very much. She would also miss her sensual workout with her close friend Janice. But most of all, she would miss her newly found excitement at The Club which she had only recently opened.

Her niece and housemate, Sophie, worked at a horse stud and accepted reduced hours and looked forward to doing baby things at home. Because she and Mary lived next door to Helen and Freddy, the two households would have access to each other when needed. And of course, Freddy was to be the father of Sophie's as yet unborn child.

Alice and Frey both lamented the loss of work in their jobs as school counsellors. They both loved their jobs. Both were pregnant and accepted they would be forced to spend more time at home together.

Like most of the others, they had their favourite sex toys for when they weren't knitting baby clothes or doing jigsaw puzzles. And like so many women in lockdown, they visited female friendly porn sites online. The two decided that they would always share these internet session and happily parked themselves on the sofa, transmitting the websites from their phones to the giant television set via a magic little box. This meant that the images were so big that they felt they were in the same room and this proved most enjoyable on many occasions.

Bertie and Rosa were the older folk who were most vulnerable to the virus. They were happy to be isolated although Bertie complained that he would miss his fortnightly get together for coffee and cake with Freddy and Roger.

Bertie complained that he still had much to say on the subject of breaking down the worlds dependance on the "couples model" as he called it.

"Nothing good will happen while we maintain this ridiculous habit of pairing off for life. Firstly, in over half the cases, it doesn't work and people separated or divorced.

"Secondly, it was obvious that people who stayed in these relationships were deeply frustrated by the repressive demands on them of constantly answering to another person.

"Thirdly, paternity and property ownership where the only reasons this system was maintained and with the likely end of democracy as we know it looming, house prices and pension funds and equity investments were likely to collapse.

"And I haven't even mentioned the problems of religion and religious wars."

Rosa looked at him. She loved him dearly but managed always to call him out.

"You haven't mentioned love once."

"Sex and love are two seperate things, my dear. We both know that."

Most of the close friends and relatives knew that Rosa and Bertie had broken up many years ago and taken lovers. Rosa entered relationships with her close girl friends and occasionally, a man.

Sometime later, she and Bertie got back together as a couple, but both maintained their freedom to embark on other relationships if they so chose, and this arrangement worked very well. It wasn't that they were desperate to take on other romantic adventures, but just knowing that they were free to do so, made the difference. They broke up after almost twenty years and had now been together for nearly fifty years.

"It was a necessary pause," agreed the two of them, lovingly.

It was Desley who had the most to lose but she wasn't particularly put out. The Club had to close only two short months after opening and only a few weeks after Desley had formed a partnership with her friend Sally who had opened The Dunking venue. The Dunking was closed too.

Desley welcomed the opportunity to take a rest and review everything about the club and the new venture and be ready to make any necessary changes or recommendations to Sally when they eventually reopened.

She and her partner Alvie, lived on the premises. Alvie knew about Desley's dalliances with Roger who she said she also had a soft spot for.

Desley had laughed, saying that now that they had so much time on their hands, she would endeavour to entice Roger to pop in for a threesome if Alvie didn't mind sharing. To which Alvie replied that she wanted first go.

Maria and her daughter Serina were at first, forced to stay home with grandfather Aldo and the boarder, Giorgio. They mostly worked for older people as cooks and housekeepers in the stately home of Vaucluse and Woollahra.

They successfully applied for positions with the council as carers so that they could continue working.

They both had each other and the two live-in men to play with when they felt like it plus a range of toys they enjoyed.

Maud, the owner of the music school and owner of the property at nineteen Eros Crescent found isolation difficult, severely limiting her adventures although she had managed to entertain herself with young Ashton and Damian after the two became suddenly sexually aware after falling prey to pizza nights with Jessica and Edith.

And Sylvia and Stella, the two girl who she had enjoyed briefly when they stayed over on the night of her house warming party, seducing Maude with the help their bunny outfits, had booked in for music classes and accomodation the week before lockdown. Maud reasoned that maybe life wouldn't be too bad after all.

———

Peoples attitudes were changed in part by the arrival of the pandemic.

Australia was fortunate that it could close its borders and clamp down easily on travel.

Europe was badly affected and Britain failed in the early stages to take action which might have prevented many of the casualties they suffered.

The USA continued to be the sad case that it had slowly become.

Big enough to make loud noises but also it seemed, too big to be able to maintain good democratic government.

It was presided over by a man who couldn't cope with an enemy he couldn't see and he couldn't lash out at, or orally deride.

The arrival of the invisible virus was to prove his undoing.

———

Life on Eros Crescent went on. The residents continued to love each other in many different ways and despite the sudden disruption of the pandemic, there was a feeling of optimism in the air.

Babies were on the way and new life called out for new ideas. And new ideas about how society worked were desperately needed.

Cross your sanitised fingers everyone, and hope.

EPILOGUE

IN A MATRIARCHAL STRUCTURE, such as exists in some tribes in South India, women have natural confidence in their own womanhood. They know their importance and that they are different from men in a special way, and this does not imply any inferiority. They are able to assert their human existence and being in a natural way.

So writes Marie Louise Von Franz in her book, *The Feminine in Fairy Tales.*

One should acknowledging Lilith, known by some as the Queen of the Night and by others as the ancient bad girl.

Lilith was said to have been Adams first wife. She was not happy with him and left. Her reasons included him always making her lie underneath him when making love and also demanding her complete obedience.

Eve replaced her and later Lilith was often represented in art by the serpent. (*See the sculpture at the entrance of Notre Dame cathedral depicting Adam and Eve, and Lilith as a serpent.*)

CONTACT

Publisher or review enquiries should include your full name and details in all correspondence.

Email:
countrynotebook@gmail.com

RICHARD LEE PUBLISHING

Erotic Fiction

New 2022:

Wet Dreams for Oldies 1: Never feel lonely again (P/back)

ISBN: 978-0-909431-23-5

Wet Dreams for Oldies 1: Never feel lonely again (H/back)

ISBN: 978-0-909431-40-2

Wet Dreams for Oldies 2: Never feel lonely again (P/back)

ISBN: 978-0-909431-24-2

The Eros Crescent trilogy as paperbacks or ebooks:

The Fifi Code

ISBN - 978-0-909431-02-0

Eros Crescent

ISBN - 978-0-909431-05-1

Mount Eros

ISBN - 978-0-909431-08-2

Excerpts from the Eros Crescent series as paperbacks or ebooks:

Janice: A sexual enigma

ISBN - 978-0-909431-10-5

Jessica: A young woman's journey

ISBN - 978-0-909431-13-6

Helen: Enough is not enough

ISBN - 978-0-909431-14-3

Maria: Always available

ISBN - 978-0-909431-15-0

Mary: Catching up

ISBN - 978-0-909431-11-2

The Club: Ladies love it!

ISBN - 978-0-909431-11-2

Happy Honeypots: Swinging in Harmony

ISBN - 978-0-909431-20-4

Roger: Ladies love to pay him

ISBN - 978-0-909431-21-1

Literary Fiction

Australian Short Stories

ISBN - 978-0-909431-00-6

Restless: A novel about two young men growing up

in Australia between 1900 and 1936 (Publication date not set.)

Memoir

The Kite Makers: Six years of a child's war - Britain 1939-1945 Anita Sinclair.

ISBN - 978-0-909431-16-7

Reference

Ducks for Starters: A Practical Guide to

Backyard Duck Keeping by Bruce Wicking

ISBN - 978-0-909431-18-1

Out of Print Titles

Mathematics for Young Children by Helen Western

ISBN - 978-0-909431-01-3

Currajong: For Those Whom Schools Have Failed

by Bruce Wicking

ISBN - 978-0-909431-03-7

The Puppetry Handbook by Anita Sinclair

ISBN - 978-0-909431-04-4

Wordswork by Chris Davidson & Bruce Wicking

ISBN - 978-0-909431-06-8

Sheep Production by Murray Elliott

ISBN - 978-0-909431-07-5

Sweethearts by Colin Talbot - *ISBN - 978-1-875207-02-2*

www.ingramcontent.com/pod-product-compliance
Lightning Source LLC
Chambersburg PA
CBHW031319120626
46554CB00001BA/470